For my best five

Jane

Catherine Jonathan Michael and Lily

Love's Illusion by Ian Waters

Copyright © 2023 Ian Waters

ISBN 9798397962254

LOVE'S ILLUSION

This is book two of the trilogy:

"It's The Human Condition"

CONTENTS

THE LOST THIRTY-TWO STOREY BOOGIE

It was a drunken New Year's Eve party in one of the top floor flats of a thirty-two-storey tower block. One of four identical blocks. Four concrete and glass lego-like structures. Although monstrosities would be a more accurate description. And situated on top of the highest hill overlooking the city as well. As subtle as a car crash.

They stood as a monument to the worst of 1960s public housing. Guaranteed to be demolished in twenty years or so – if they didn't fall down first, of course. God alone knows what the architects and planners thought they were doing back then.

Or perhaps they weren't thinking at all. Maybe their 'creativity' was born out of an excess of high-grade coke or other Class A narcotic. Not that they cared, of course, not when they all lived in huge semis or detached houses with gardens all around. But the modernist, brutalist architecture was ample good enough for the lower orders in society, or so they thought.

Anyway.

It was two o'clock in the morning and the party had warmed up nicely. Most of those present were drunk, but pleasantly so. Almost everybody knew everybody else and since they were all of an age, the atmosphere was relaxed and friendly. A few were dancing in a loose, drunken sort of way, but one couple were dancing close and slow.

At the end of the second record, the woman leaned back and looked at the man she was dancing with. And it wasn't a pleasant look.

"What's going on here, Kenneth Roberts? Eh? That's what I want to know. And d'you know where William's got to? I haven't seen him for a while."

William? That's her husband. Billy or Bill to the rest of us of course. My best mate and the questions came from his wife after we were two dances in.

Which question to answer first? Take the safer of the two options, I thought.

"Bill? I think he's gone downstairs with Joe to get some more drink from his place. We're running a bit short here."

"He's been a long time," she says. "Joseph only lives downstairs."

"Yes, but come on, it *is* twenty floors down and the lifts aren't working again. Bound to take them a while," he says. With a straight face.

"Hmmm. I never know when you're being honest with me, Kenneth Roberts." She studies his face and moves her hips in even closer.

I just shrug in response. Nothing else I can say to this woman who always uses both my names when she's in full interrogation mode. As she was that night. Apart from my mother, Carol Miles was the only person who ever called me Kenneth. I was 'Kenny' to everybody else, but she thought that shortening names was "common". And that tells you all you need to know about her, really.

She was far from being the sharpest knife in the box but she wasn't completely unaware. Plus she had a *very* suspicious nature. She could smell conspiracies a mile off and her antennae were in high twitch mode that night.

"Not being honest with you? What do you mean, Carol?" I say as I pull away slightly and look her in the eye. My voice and face all innocence. But she isn't buying it at all. I was guilty of something; she was convinced of that. And she wasn't about to let it go.

"What I *mean* is, you're my William's best friend yet you've never, ever, danced with me before, Kenneth Roberts. And now it's two in a row. Slow ones as well. So something's going on, I just can't work out what."

I give her my best, most sincere smile and try to inject some humour.

"Aah, just relax and enjoy it, Carol. After all, it's not often I give a girl more than one dance at a time. I have to ration them because they just can't control themselves otherwise."

"God, your chat up lines are as bad as ever… but I have to say your control's pretty good." That sly, nastiness, creeps into her eyes. "I can't feel anything down there," she says, giving me a bump and grind with her hips.

I manage to control the shudder. Get an erection dancing with *you*? More chance if I was dancing with a corpse. You just stay right where you are good boy, I thought. Nice and relaxed. Because if you stand to attention any time in the next ten minutes I'll walk outside and throw myself off the balcony.

And it's not that she was physically unattractive. Because she wasn't. She was quite stunning in fact. Beautiful face and a body that men lusted after and women envied. And she dressed to show it off. Like that night. Low-cut top, short skirt and high heels. High enough so that our eyes were on a level.

7

So it wasn't anything physical that caused me and many others to dislike her, it was the person she was. There was something about her personality that I, we, found almost repellent. She displayed a complete lack of warmth, kindness and humanity. Probably couldn't even spell 'empathy'. And I have never been attracted to narcissists.

Nevertheless, I take a deep breath and hold her in for the third dance in a row because I'd given my word. But he owes me big time for this one.

Meanwhile: Over in the corner by the door.

"How's it going then Dave? You okay?"

"Eh? Oh, evening John. Yes, all good, nothing bad, mate. You?"

"Yeah fine. Now I've recovered from climbing those bloody stairs that is. Bloody lifts're knackered again. Thirty-two flights? We drank half the sodding beer on the way up. But worth it though. Look out the windows and you could be in a plane. Amazing. And a good party, eh? You want a fresh can?"

"Nah, you're alright, mate. I'm okay for now. Got one here and a backup on the table there. But there is something you might be able to help me with, though," he said. "You can explain it to me maybe because I can't for the life of me work it out. See that?"

"See what exactly?" John says glancing around the room.

"That. I don't want to point, but over there, by the sofa? Kenny dancing with Bill's wife. See them?"

John nods as they both watch the couple slowly turning in time to the music.

"Yeah, I see them. But so what, Dave? They're only dancing."

"Yes, but real slow ones. And it ain't the first one.

"No?"

He's been dancing with her for a while now, two or three records at least. And getting stuck right in as well. Look at him!"

"I dunno mate, maybe she's getting stuck into him?"

"Her? Don't think so somehow. But you've got to admit it's weird."

"Yes, I know," John says with a grin. "And you don't know why? I thought all the guys knew. How've you not heard?"

"Eh? No. Heard what? All I know for sure is he can't stand the woman and she doesn't like him much either. Mind you, far as I can tell, she doesn't like anybody much except herself."

The two of them laugh, acknowledging the truth of it.

"And she reckons he leads Bill astray. That's a good one, eh? Him leading *Bill* astray? That's like saying Goebbels led Hitler astray. Like I said, all I know is they can't stand each other so I just can't figure it out."

"Yeah, but I can," John says, grinning. "We all can - apart from you, that is."

"Yeah?"

"Yes we can."

"Oh, right... what you were saying about all the guys knowing. Come on then, tell me what's going on between the two of them?"

"Okay. You ready for this?" John asks. "Kenny's dancing with her so Bill can get his end away."

"*What?* What the hell are you on about?" Dave says, totally confused.

"You deaf or what? So Bill can get his end away, I said. Give his girlfriend one. You know the latest one? That tasty piece from work he's having it off with? The one whose husband's always away playing table-tennis and cricket?"

"Oh yeah, the dark-haired one with the body? Very tasty she is... but hang on, he can't be away playing on New Year's Eve, though. Table tennis, indoors, maybe, but not exactly a winter sport, cricket, is it?"

"You've got her, Dave," John says, twirling his finger around his right temple. "The crazy one. Might even be too much for Bill to handle if he's not careful. And I heard her tell somebody her old man's sick or something. Some stomach bug, so he couldn't make it. Well she's here tonight, her husband's not and she's dying for it. Bill is as well of course, so she asks him what's he going to do about? Has he got any balls or what?

"Oh what? She any idea what Bill's like when he's given a challenge?"

"Oh, I'm pretty sure she does, yes," John says, nodding. "She's known him long enough. So anyway, he asks Kenny to dance with his missus, four or five records or so, fifteen minutes maybe. Then I agreed to take her into the kitchen and get her a drink while Kenny lets him know the coast's clear and they can come back in. All that so he can give her one. Rob was all for snapping them with the polaroid for a laugh like..."

Dave stared at him. "You have *got* to be joking, my son."

"No, no. Seriously now. He was going to. Until we reminded him what Bill would likely do to him if he did. Asked him if he thought a Polaroid camera would fit up his backside or not."

"And that would be the least of it. Because you say *she's* crazy, but Bill's mental. Always was. But he's taking a helluva a risk, she could walk into the bedroom any time."

"Maybe so, but they don't have to worry about that because they're not in the bedroom are they? That's the best thing about it. See, they're…"

"Not in the bathroom, surely? That's just as bad, somebody's bound…"

"Nope. Wrong again, Dave. It's absolutely brilliant this one. Best ever. You'd never guess in a million years. What it is, see, they're not in the flat at all."

"Not in the flat? How? Where then? Oh no, not in the bloody lifts, for Christ's sake."

John laughs. "No. The *lifts*? Gimme a break. And anyway, they're not working tonight so how could they get in one?"

"So where then? I can't…."

"If you'd shut your mouth for a minute and give me a chance, I'll tell you. No, I'll give you a clue first. They're only about ten feet away from us right now."

"*Whaat?*" Dave stared at him, puzzled. He looked around the room and shook his head. "No, that's impossible. No way."

"Straight up, less than ten feet away."

"Whaat?"

"You've an amazing vocabulary Dave, you know that? Nobody would ever guess you'd been to Uni."

"Yeah, yeah, very bloody funny. Stop messing me about and just tell me."

11

"You'll never believe this, Dave, but they're right outside there, just behind the curtains, on the balcony!"

"You *what?* The fucking *balcony?* You're winding me up now."

"No I'm not. The two of them are out there. They are. Straight up... at least it will be he hopes. They're standing on that tiny little balcony. What do they call it again, a Juliet balcony?"

"But out on the *balcony?* Jesus Christ, John, it's December. It's bloody freezing out there. Seriously. And we're thirty-two storeys up!"

"Well, yeah, but they're not exactly going to strip off, are they? It's a quickie, a stand-up job. If it'll stand up at all in this weather that is."

"He's got some balls though, I'll say that for him."

"Yeah, you're right because I wouldn't fancy mine hangin' out in that weather tonight."

"No, I don't mean *that.* I meant him doing it the way he is. With his wife here."

"Oh! Yeah, right enough, I suppose."

"It's terrible really though."

"What is, Dave?"

"Him. What he's doing. When you think about it I mean. It's awful that is. Screwing his girlfriend with his wife no more than six feet away."

"And? What's your point, Dave?"

"What? You don't think that's bad?"

John smiles. "Cheating on his wife, you mean, lying to her all the time? Course I think that's bad. But he screws his piece when they're away with work together, going to meetings in London and such..."

"Yeah, maybe, but that's different."

12

"How is it? What are you on about different? Look, it's the same thing, no? He's screwing around, cheating on his wife. She hasn't a clue he's doing it, so it doesn't actually matter *where* he does it. Screws her there, screws her here, how's it any different?"

"I don't know John, it just is."

"Bollocks."

"No, it is… in fact what he's doing now is way worse."

"But it's *isn't*, Dave. Not at all. Don't you get it? It's no different in principle. And it's the principle that's important here. The morality of it. Look, if you're going to screw around on your wife in the first place, what difference does it make if you're six hundred miles or six feet away? Really. Think about it. It's *doing* it that's wrong, isn't it? Not *where* you do it. The where doesn't actually matter."

"Well I think it's wrong, the bastard."

"There you go then. If you think it's wrong, then it's wrong. Wherever it's done. End of. So there isn't any difference is there? Tonight's not really any worse than all the other nights, is it? Okay, so he's taking a much bigger risk, doing it as close as this. But that's all it is, the risk. Not a question of whether it's worse or not. Right?"

"But… No, you're right I suppose… fuck it, yes, you *are* right. When you put it like that, it's no different at all. I'd never thought of it like that. Cheers for that John."

"No problem. See you later. Pray for me 'cos I'm just off to take that woman into the kitchen for a drink so Kenny can escape and give Bill the nod."

LOVE IN THE BOTTOMLANDS

It was Christmas time in South London. For some reason I still can't recall, my friend and his wife were staying in London rather than travelling home to their families for the festivities. Likewise, I had decided not to go back home either and my girlfriend at the time was happy with that.

Come over to us, we said. A meal, a few drinks (well…) kip over or get a taxi back. Whatever. Which they did. Meal over, my friend Bob and I then embraced an ancient male tradition… we wandered off into the night to find a pub, leaving the women to themselves. Strangely, they somehow didn't seem too bothered about that. But hey, we left them enough drink, *and* there was a telly to watch - once they'd done the dishes of course. Ha!

We strolled on out but instead of turning right towards the pub under the railway bridge and the friendly laid-back West Indians, we went left. Wandered through the back end of Clapham because the area consisted of rows and rows of Victorian terraces, each street, it seemed, with its own pub. The ideal set up I thought for a serious pub crawl. Lots of hostelries but very little walking to be done in between. Perfect!

We crossed over the main road on a normal London winter night, turned a corner - and found we'd crossed over into the netherworld.

"Who turned the fucking lights out?" Bob asked. A not unreasonable question because it had suddenly become very, dark. Very, very, dark indeed.

"Sorry, man," I said, "I had absolutely no idea they'd started developing this part of the area."

"*This* part? *Eh?* You do realise you've taken us back to Berlin in nineteen forty-five!"

Bit of an exaggeration, that because lots of the nicer terraces were left untouched, but yeah, okay, we'd walked right into the bit, the bigger bit, they'd started on. And '*started*' was right. All they'd done was pull down the houses. Nothing else.

The roads and pavements were pretty much intact apart from a few cracks and breaks from the demolition vehicles, but almost all the houses were completely flattened. One or two sort of half remained, standing at weird angles like blackened teeth, silhouetted against the sky.

And there were no streetlights left in this part at all. The moon was the only light we had as we stared at a scene that was, to be fair, pretty reminiscent, if not of 1945 Berlin, certainly of London in the blitz. A complete wasteland. A completely *dark* wasteland. We thought about turning back – we weren't scared, you understand, we just couldn't see a pub – but decided to go through it all just in case we could find a pub. Any pub. Anywhere.

So we stumbled on over cracked pavements, piles of brick and rubble and the remains of bonfires where they'd been burning floorboards, staircases and rafters. We were feeling more and more isolated and strange until Bob said he'd spotted lights in the distance. I had serious doubts about that but nevertheless, I peered across to where his finger was pointing.

Yes! Glory be! One building was still proudly standing. *And* there were lights in the windows. As we approached, we realised it was a pub. A Youngs pub. And a full one at that given the sound and the music coming from it. Quite spooky it was.

15

But when we got there, the door was locked, with a notice on it telling us the pub was closed for a private party. People from the now-demolished terraces were having a last night in their old boozer because it due to be pulled down the next day. I turned to leave but Bob wasn't to be deterred. He just couldn't ignore a find like this. He knocked on the door.

The man who answered pointed to the notice and told him sorry, son, but it's a private party. Only old residents allowed. He said it politely, but very firmly. Disappointed, I turned and walked away until I realised Bob wasn't with me. I looked back and saw he was deep in conversation with the man.

Next thing I heard Bob calling me. Gesturing for me to come back and come on in! I have no idea what he'd said, but his silver tongue had worked its magic again. It was one of the most impressive performances I'd ever witnessed from him. And given his previous record, that is high praise indeed.

We followed the man inside and there we happily spent the rest of the night. One Glaswegian and one Geordie in the middle of a hundred or so born and bred residents of a tiny part of South London. Shoulder to shoulder. A free bar, a piano player, and enough soloists to last the night. Stuff your karaoke, these people were used to singing in pubs and were more than competent.

I was handed the first of many drinks I was given that night. Took a mouthful and then felt a tap on the shoulder.

"'Ello love. And who are you then? Not seen you before. You ain't local are ya?"

I turned and looked at a smiling woman who was very happily drunk. She must have been in her sixties and was dressed for a wedding, hat and all. I explained who we were, where I lived and how we happened to be there.

"*Oooh,* you sound just like him on the telly! Love 'is voice I do. But are you a likely lad as well?" she asked with a wink. Then grabbed my arms.

"C'mere, darlin', gissa kiss."

So I did. Well, it would have seemed churlish not to. But I didn't actually give *her* a kiss. No, she kissed *me.* And I do mean kissed. Not cheeks or lips or anything polite like that. No, it was a full on, mouth open, tongue kiss. And when certain of her friends saw us, they demanded the same. How could I refuse? When I came up for air, they were red-faced and laughing.

"Ain't tasted nuffink as young as that in bleedin' years," one of them said.

And they all fell about. If anybody was watching, they didn't seem to care. Because it wasn't serious. Nothing that night was. It was just fun for everybody, and love being shared amongst everybody.

So we chatted, laughed, drank and had a dance or six. And drank again. Because all the drinks were free that night. "*Bin fiddlin' the stock for months,*" the Landlord said. As a result, many drinks were handed to us by people we'd never met before and would never meet again. People talked to us as if we were long-lost nephews returned from the colonies.

Something to do with tales Bob was spinning inside his web of alcohol-fuelled charm perhaps? Almost certainly. I didn't give it a second thought. Just carried on chatting, drinking and sharing even more drunken kisses with the older women who were there.

Husbands? Boyfriends? If there were any present, they didn't seem to mind. And laughing and drinking until my senses were scrambled and my brain porridge. All of which made it one of the great little nights, though. And all the better for being totally unplanned and unexpected.

Before we left, the Landlord presented us each with a Youngs Brewery lapel pin and, amazingly, a wooden crate filled with twelve bottles of Youngs Special. For free! His stock-fiddling must have been on an epic scale.

Carrying the case of beer between us and the love we'd received within us, we attempted to find our way back to the flat. Turn right? Turn Left? Who knows? Or cares. We picked one… and promptly got lost. We wandered unsteadily along some unfamiliar back streets, stopping every so often to put the case of beer down so we could light cigarettes.

Until eventually we came upon a Police Station. A very 1950s Dixon of Dock Green type police station it has to be said. Built of old London brick with tall black iron railings and sandstone steps leading up to the front door. Above which, suspended on curved iron arms, hung the iconic blue lamp with single word, 'POLICE' written on it in bold white letters.

The dislocating sense of having stepped back in time was heightened when we saw a police constable, a very large police constable, in full uniform, buttons all brightly polished and pointy helmet sitting squarely on his head, make his way slowly down the steps and stand in front of us on the pavement. Almost surreal.

He didn't look friendly at all, just gave us the old, stern, up-and-down look. Taking in the sight of two grinning idiots with a case of beer between their legs.

In my drunken state, I was half-expecting to hear him utter the classic policeman's words: *"Ello, 'ello, 'ello. And what's all this 'ere then?"*

I was pretty close as it turned out. What he actually said was:

"Evenin' chaps, and what's that you're got there, eh? Beer is it?"

We agreed that it was. To be fair, it was pretty hard to deny, when there were a dozen bottles of beer peering out of a wooden crate with "Young's Brewery" stamped on the side.

"Glad we can agree on that, lads" he said. "Care to tell me exactly where you got it from and where you might be taking it to?"

So we explained. Who we were. Where I lived. The night wander to find a pub or two. Discovering we'd walked into the bottomlands. Coming across the only pub left standing and how we'd been welcomed in by the locals. We didn't explain it quite as succinctly as that, you understand, drink having taken its toll on our ability to articulate it precisely. But he seemed to get it because he visibly relaxed and became almost friendly.

"Ah, yes. I'm just off there meself. I've been the beat copper round here for years. I know them all, parents, kids and grandkids, so they invited me over for the last night. Insisted I wear me full uniform. Still going are they?"

Yes, indeed they are, we said. And since they were taking orders for fried breakfasts as we left, we suspect they'll be going right through till morning. Not that there'll be that many left standing by then, we added, not the way they were going at it.

"Don't you worry about that," he said, "a lot of 'em will still be going this time tomorrow night. Can hold their drink that lot." He laughed. "Shouldn't be at all surprised if they don't invite the demolition men in to join them tomorrow."

We explained that we were completely lost and asked him if he could give us directions. Which he was more than happy to do.

"Best write them down for you, eh? Alcohol does have a tendency to affect the memory I've found."

Which was a very polite way of saying that us piss-heads wouldn't remember a word he said and were likely to end up in Wimbledon or somewhere. And write them down he duly did - in block capitals – having torn out the last page from his little black policeman's notebook.

"Well, best be on me way now," he said with a smile as he touched fingers to the brim of his helmet. "Safe journey home you chaps. Night."

And off he went with his steady policeman's stride. And off we also went, following his clear and precise directions. Which enabled us to make our stumbling way back to the flat. Where we discovered the two ladies were in much the same drunken condition as we were, despite not having walked The Bottomlands. And the dishes had been done. *And* they still loved us.

And just in case you're wondering, yes, I still have the Youngs lapel pin. But we drank the beer.

FAMILY GUY

The three men walked down Charing Cross Road together, the two older ones devouring their first after-work cigarettes. They stopped by the entrance to Leicester Square Tube Station, moving closer together while streams of people weaved and snaked around them without complaint, as London tube travellers do. And without making any physical contact either. Like human bats disappearing underground.

Charles, the oldest of the three, in his middle fifties, ground his cigarette out under his shoe and glanced across the road.

"Coming for a pint, then, Mike?" he asked the man in the three-piece blue suit, the only one still wearing a tie. "Max and I are having a quick couple before we head off home."

Mike smiled and shook his head. "Sorry guys, but I know *your* quick couple. Sorry, but I'm off home," he said. "Lydia's cooking a Lasagne tonight and it wouldn't do to turn up late smelling of beer and Whisky. Gotta pick up a decent bottle of red on the way. Enjoy anyway. See you Monday, guys."

He turned and walked down the steps into the Station. Charles and Max crossed the road and walked back up the other side before disappearing into the bar of the Bear and Staff. It was already filling up with the after-work crowd and the serving area was full. But they were regulars, and good tippers, so the barman served them immediately, ignoring the complaints of others who'd been waiting for a while.

"Usual?" he asked, not bothering to wait for a reply before he pulled two pints of bitter. The two men allowed them to settle then finished a third of their pints with the first mouthful. They then made their way through the crowd, and out into Bear Street where they lit fresh cigarettes.

They stood smoking, taking the occasional bite out of their pints while indulging in the ancient pastime of watching the girls go by. They were comfortable in the silence of regular, seasoned, drinking companions and their pints were almost finished before either of them spoke.

"He's a miserable bastard, isn't he?" Max said.

"Who is? Charles asked as he followed the progress of a very tight, short skirt. "Mike, you mean?"

"Yeah," Max said. "Tosser. Never stays for a drink, does he? Always got some reason for running off home to the little wife. And what sort of name is that anyway, *Lydia?* Is she foreign or what?"

Charles shook his head and started to say something but Max just carried on speaking.

"Mine would wonder what the hell was going on if I turned up before half seven. 'Specially on a Friday. Got her well trained I have. And what is he, twenty six or something? Bit young to be ball and chained like that. Tosser."

"You ever seen her?" Charles asked.

"Yeah, once," Max said. "She turned up to a Christmas party, only one, mind you. What about it?"

"Once should've been enough, even for you Max. She's absolutely stunning. Sexy as hell, that's what. And bright as well, which is a real bonus. If I had her waiting at home for me I wouldn't be standing here now, that's for sure."

"Yeah, I suppose you're right there… but even so, he's still a tosser."

Charles was silent for a while. "Tell me something Max, what's our business?"

"Our business? What are you on about? It's Insurance of course, What…"

Charles shook his head. "No," he said. That's where you're wrong, Max. It *used* to be Insurance, but it's not anymore. Today, Insurance is just the content, the dross work drones like us do. The *business* is Information Technology - IT."

"Well yes, we *use* IT, I mean…"

"No. Again, we *used* to. First it was some big, fat, remote database that spewed out hard copy info that was supposed to be useful. But was always a bit too late to be *really* useful. Then we got terminals, dumb terminals though, on the desktop so we could access the database ourselves and get some info that was just a bit more relevant and timely."

"Yes I get all that," Max said, "but…."

"Don't think you *do* get it, Max. Because what you don't get any more is what's happened since the Internet. The World Wide Web changed everything. To the extent that the whole business, right from the Board on down to the case teams, depend on the IT platform, the systems, and the Internet, for absolutely *everything* we do these days. Communication with clients, partners, customers, *everybody,* is done on the web. All our documentation, cases, instructions, management information, finance, accounts, everything, is web-based."

He paused for a moment to take another drink, wondering whether to continue his lecture. Yes, why not, he thought, Max really needs to understand this stuff.

"Christ, Max, even our internal telecoms are system-based now. Work through the PCs. No, I'm telling you, we couldn't survive more than a few days without properly functioning IT. We could lose the Chairman, The CEO, the whole bloody Board and it would have less impact than if our IT went belly-up."

He took yet another mouthful of his pint. "As for you and me, we could disappear under a bus and they'd replace us in a matter of hours. There's thousands like us, workhorses, only got to where we are because we've worked in the same business since we left school. Experience is all we've got to offer and that's worth sod all these days."

"Not at all," Max said. "What *are* you on about? We could easily get a job with another Insurance company."

"At our age? Just how bloody dumb are you Max? We'd put in our CVs – that we'd have to write in the first place, of course. They'd take one look at those numbers, fifty-three and fifty-five, and sling our applications straight in the bin. Christ Max, most of the guys doing our jobs in other companies are twenty years younger than us. We'd be lucky to get jobs driving bloody mini-cabs at night in North London."

"Yeah, okay, but supposing you *are* right, all the IT guys could be replaced just as easily, couldn't they?"

"No, not like we could. Our systems are bespoke and our guys know them inside out. Take quite a while to find anybody who's got the same mixture of dinosaur and contemporary web-based computing that our guys have. And by the time we did find them the business would be on its bloody knees."

"Okay, okay," Max said, "you've explained the situation to me *Professor*, but what's your point? About Mike, I mean".

"Point is, Max, you agree with me how business critical our IT is…."

"God's sake, yes!"

"And how much constant pressure there is on the IT guys?

"Yes."

"So, given all that, especially the pressure, tell me, Max, when do you ever see Mike unhappy? When do you ever see him stressed, drink too much, stuff his face with junk food all day? Complain about senior bloody management all the time. Shout at people. Lose it over big things, or even little things in the office?"

Max pondered for a moment. "Now you come to mention it, I don't think I have," Max said.

Charles paused and finished his pint. "And those things I've just described, all those little behaviours, any of them ring a bell with you by any chance?"

"Ah," Max said, slowly nodding his head, "good point, Charles, well made. Could be talking about us, you mean."

Well, you at least, Charles thought.

"And you haven't seen him do any of those things because he never does. Fact. He's always Mr Cool. Staff love him, and that's all the staff, not just his. Especially the women. And why's that? Because he's always got time for people. He shows them respect, whatever level they're at."

"But he's a terrible bloody flirt," Max said. "Dunno how he gets away with it all the time. They'd complain to Personnel if we tried it."

"He gets away with it, as you put it, for a couple of reasons. Firstly, because he's a *very* good-looking young guy who's always well-dressed. Secondly, and much more importantly, he flirts in exactly the same way with all the women. Senior or junior. Young, old, fat, thin, beautiful or ugly, he flirts with them all the same way. Notices their hair, clothes, shoes, whatever and pays them little compliments about how they look. But never, ever, touches them..."

"But that's still what the call sexist, these days, isn't it?" Max said, "Even if he doesn't actually touch them?"

"No. Because of the way he does it. Women know the difference between lechers and men who are simply paying old fashioned compliments, trust me."

"Still…"

"*And* he takes as long as he needs to explain things, even to the numpties," Charles said. *Always* does. Never makes them feel stupid. *Never* says he's too busy. *And* he respects them for their abilities, asks them for their input and trusts them to do their jobs without constantly looking over their shoulders. Even today, most guys don't treat women like that."

"Hmmm, yes, I did notice he's got more than his fair share of women working for him," Max said. "Thought IT was for blokes meself."

Charles rolled his eyes and decided to give up on that one. Some definitely fall on stony ground. He thought.

"Look, Max, he's always in a good mood, always relaxed. And he shouldn't be, doesn't deserve to be, he's the bloody IT Manager. Hardware, systems, network, helpdesk, the bloody lot. *Nightmare* bloody job that is."

He wiggled his empty glass. "Given all that, Max, you tell me exactly who the complete tossers are, eh? Young Mike, off for a nice Lasagne, good red wine and a nice, warm, beautiful wife afterwards on the clean Egyptian cotton? Or maybe it's us, eh? Sad old bastards drinking for hours just to put off going home to microwaved mush, cheap plonk and our much chillier wives?"

Max finished his drink without replying and turned to Charles.

"Another, before you start sounding off again, depressing me even more?" he asked.

"Yeah," Charles said, with a resigned shake of the head "Pint. And a Jack Daniels. Make it a large one."

* * * *

Half an hour later Mike stepped off the train at Earls Court and turned right down the Earls Court Road. He walked into a small shop with an Off Licence attached and came out carrying a decent bottle of Chianti Classico and a lemon and sultana cheesecake. He walked back towards the Underground station then took a left into Penywern Road and rang the bell of a basement flat.

The door was opened by a tiny, slim, woman in her early forties, wearing a silk kimono that came only part way down her thighs. She wore no makeup except for dark red lipstick and her natural brown hair was cut in a short, straight bob with a heavy fringe.

"Hey!" Mike said. "Love the new cut. *Very* old-school Sassoon. You never had it like that when you worked for God. All twin sets, semi-perm and sensible shoes you were then. Took me quite a while to appreciate what was going on underneath all that."

"Funny, you've never mentioned that before," she said. "So tell me, when exactly *did* you begin to appreciate it?"

"One of the days God took us to the pub at lunchtime. You were sitting at the end of the bench seat and I noticed you'd changed your sensible shoes for a pair of kitten heels. *Then* I saw you'd crossed your legs and your skirt had tightened over your thigh and I spotted the little bumps that indicated suspenders. And when I noticed *that*, I thought to myself, *hello!* there's a lot more to this woman than meets the eye if she wears stockings and suspenders in this day and age. Especially to work."

She smiled and shook her head. "What is it with you men and your stockings? Doesn't matter what age, it gets you all."

"Ah, that. There's probably psychologists written learned papers about it. I just know they turn me on. Always have. It attracted me at the time but didn't do anything about it for a while because I'd never had any kind of sign that you fancied me at all."

"Such a shame," she said.

"Yeah, maybe, but I haven't yet reached that desperate age when guys just dive in when there's no signals coming out. And I'm not like a lot of guys who just because they fancy themselves, they think every woman wants to fall into bed with them as soon as they're asked."

She smiled again and kissed him lightly on the cheek.

"Which is part of your appeal, you lovely man. You're not in love with yourself and you don't *try* all the time. But you shouldn't have waited so long. My bad as well though," she said. "I should have given you some signals because I fancied you long before that day in the pub. I was way ahead of you."

"Really?"

"Really. The first time I saw you without your jacket, in those tight suit trousers you wore I thought, *'Now there's a lovely bum if ever I saw one. And pair of thighs. Wouldn't mind getting my hands on all that.'* How did they get to be so well-developed?" she asked. You do some sport?"

"Cycling," he said. "I've cycled, seriously, since my early teens. Played, football, tennis and cricket as well."

She smiled. "Well thank the lord for the humble bicycle and male ball sports is all I can say. And that was when I decided I should try for it."

She saw his look of surprise and laughed out loud.

'What? You think women don't look at men's bodies in a sexual way? The way you men do with women? I've got news for you, young man. We do more often than you know. I wanted to see for myself what you were all about. And, unlike you, I did something about it."

"And thank god you did," he said. "I'm not sure I'd ever have chanced it if you hadn't given me that post-it with your phone number and *'call me when you leave tonight'* written under it." He laughed. "It made me feel like I was fifteen and back in class again."

"That's what I thought. You were obviously interested but not making a move, so I decided to do it instead. Worked out quite well for both of I'd say," she whispered as she kissed him on the mouth. Then lifted her head away.

29

"And my hair bloody-well should look good. You were quite right about the style. Vidal Sassoon trained my sweet boy is. Costs an arm and a leg. But worth it. And God would never have appreciated a secretary looking like this. He wanted grey and boring, like the rest of you lot, all grey suits, plain ties, polished shoes and brown tongues."

"No gods in what you're doing now, though, is there?" he said. "Kept woman with your rich man buying you this flat and all the rest of your expensive gear."

"No, there's no gods," she said, "and not many heroes either. A few though, like you. Although *you* don't have to pay for me. Don't forget that."

"Not in cash, anyway," he said.

"Of course not. But don't worry, you're plenty in credit as far as I'm concerned. Plenty."

"Not as much as *him*, though, bet he's gold cards all the way."

She laughed. "But of course. What else would you expect the chairman and owner of a City finance company to have?"

"So *that's* what he is, you never said."

"You never asked… and I liked that you didn't."

"None of my business," he said. "And I'm not digging for information now. We've both got our own lives, made better by the times we spend together like this. And that's absolutely fine by me, don't need to know any more."

"No, I don't mind, Michael. I don't want to boast or, god forbid, sound complacent, but I really do have the best of all worlds. My own life with my friends, flat all paid for, kept in a style I have *definitely* not been accustomed to… and then I have you." She smiled. "A sugar-daddy *and* a gorgeous toy-boy. I ask you, what more could a poor girl want? It's the stuff of dreams."

He laughed. "Never thought of it like that. And there's no danger of the three ever coming together. But hang on... '*sugar-daddy*' you said. He older than you then?"

"He is indeed. By twenty years. But he's very fit for his age. Plays a lot of golf – I think he can walk onto the fairway at Sunningdale through his garden gate – and works out every day in his home gym. And in case you were wondering, Viagra takes care of the other, and speaking of '*the other*', come here, you," she said, grinning.

She took his hand and walked into the hallway. Halfway down she turned and embraced him, kissing him hard this time. After a minute or so, he pulled his head away, put the wine and cheesecake on the hall stand and then turned to kiss her again. He slid his hands underneath her kimono and caressed her buttocks. No pants this time, he thought.

"Before or after," he asked breaking away and nodding at the wine and cheesecake.

She raised her eyebrows and shook her head. "After," she said as he slid one hand round the front and pressed it between her legs. The clean, smoothness of her sex that always aroused him. He wished again that he could find a way to persuade Lydia to shave herself there. Or, better still, let him do it for her. Maybe. In the right mood. A post-Champagne mood maybe rather than red wine.

And she was already aroused he realised. "You got yourself ready then," he said.

She gently pulled his hand away. "Of course. Not like we've got all night, now do we? So less talking now, young man, more action."

31

She led him down the hall to the bedroom where she slid out of the kimono and began to undress him. Then giggled as she pulled him towards the bed by his erection.

"Oh my. Have to start calling you the battery boy," she said as she pushed him onto his back, climbed astride and quickly slid him inside her.

"What?" he asked.

"Ever Ready?"

"Oh, yeah," he said, closing his eyes as she started to move on him. "Very droll."

Afterwards, they sat up against the pillows sipping Chianti and eating cheesecake.

"No problem getting away then, obviously," she said as she lit a cigarette.

"No, I just feed them a line when I'm set to leave. I fed them the Lydia cooking number tonight when they asked me if I was staying for a few beers. That one always works with those two sad bastards. If you make a reference to what they haven't got, it always shuts them up. Envy, coupled with their sad imaginations, works wonders."

"And what about her? Doesn't she wonder when you get back so late?"

"Lydia? No, she just thinks I'm with them. That's what I tell her and she couldn't imagine it's anything but the truth, she's so trusting. And I've been very careful. Made sure she's never met either of them to talk to, she hasn't got their mobile numbers, so everything's cool… for at least another two hours, I'd say. Three if I really push it, but I don't like to raise any suspicions that could lead to questions and awkward discussions. I like to leave things cool for the next time. Don't want to spoil this good thing we have through momentary greed, do we?"

"Indeed not," she said. Then looked around. "Well, the cheesecake isn't getting hot and the wine isn't getting cold so why don't we have another main course before we start on the dessert?" she asked, smiling up at him as she stroked his erection.

"Help yourself, why don't you," he said with a grin.

"I always do, thank you very much. Because *this* what I like so much about you young ones," she said. "No slouching, pay firm attention all the time without any Viagra in sight."

She bit his right nipple. And then again as he gave a little gasp of pleasure.

"Interest you in another before the obligatory shower, sir? Your turn to do the work this time."

"Sounds good to me," he said, as he knelt between her thighs and entered her for a second time. Then he paused.

"What?" She asked.

"Just thinking, have to remember to get another bottle on the way home."

LOVE'S ILLUSION

Robert Allen rolled over, awake before the six o'clock alarm. He lay on his back and felt his early morning erection. His *rare* early morning erection. Smiled as he moved his hand across and stroked his wife's thigh and buttocks in silent question. A grunt, and a back-heel to the shins gave him the answer he had come to expect. Sighing, he slid out of bed and walked quietly into the bathroom.

He had showered and was shaving when he realised she was standing in the bathroom doorway watching him. She still had on one of Laura's over-sized t-shirts that she wore to bed these days and her eyes were full of sleep.

"Hi," he said, "You okay?"

"Not sure. Depends really," she said, looking down at the floor, not at him.

"Depends on what?"

"On whether now's the right time to talk about this or not."

"If you're saying that then it's not the right time."

"*Rob*....."

"Okay, okay, talk about what?"

"Whether I'm okay or not. About what's really bothering me at the moment."

"Right," he said, his heart sinking a little at the prospect of another early morning row. And carrying that into work. There had been a couple of conversations like this is recent weeks. An opening, sharp and pointed, but nothing afterwards. Ah well, never be a good time, he thought. Here goes.

"It depends on what? What do you mean?"

"Depends on whether you're having an affair or not," she said, still not looking at him.

"*What?*" He almost cut himself as he spat shaving foam onto the bathroom mirror. "*What* did you say?"

"You heard me."

He didn't reply, just shook his head, picked up a towel and wiped the foam off the mirror.

"Well," she said, when he'd finished. "Are you? Are you having an affair or not? Tell me."

"Are you for real? You seriously asking me *that?* And throwing it at me when I've a *razor* in my hand?"

"Yes I am. It was a serious question and I want an answer... think I *deserve* an answer."

"A serious answer to a serious question. That what you're saying."

"Yes. Stop prevaricating."

He turned to look at her. "I'm not prevaricating. I just don't know where the question's come from. But if you really want to know, I'll give you the only honest answer I can. No, Annie. No, I'm not having an affair. An *affair*, Jesus." He shook his head again.

"Well it feels to me like you are."

"*Feels* like I am? Eh? What the hell's that supposed to mean?"

"I get the sense is what..."

"Ah, women's intuition, is that it? *That* sort of feeling you mean."

"Stop it. Just stop and tell me!"

"I already have. I said I wasn't. Thought you were listening. Anyway, some sort of bloody affair it would be if I was. When do I get the time to have an affair, tell me that? If I'm not here, I'm at work..."

"And you're at work an awful lot these days..."

"...And you know the reason for that well enough, why I take all the extra I can get, we've got to fund Laura's Uni for four years, or had you forgotten? You're not earning at the moment so I've got to pick up the money any way I can."

She didn't speak, just shook her head and folded her arms across her breasts... and her erect nipples, he noticed. She seemed to read his thoughts - or at least follow his eyes - and reached for the robe hanging behind the bathroom door.

"What on earth made you ask that anyway?" he said. "When have I ever given you reason to even think that? How, I mean?"

"I don't know, but it's gotten worse lately. It's things I've noticed. About you, the way you've been recently."

"Things? What things? You're not making any sense here, Annie. Really. I do the same things I've always done."

"But that's exactly my point, Robert, you don't. Take that aftershave you're wearing. You've never used aftershave before. And your boxers," she said before he could respond. "Your *silk* boxers. What happened to your old Y-fronts? *And* you've lost weight. You look better than you have for years."

He stared at her but she didn't speak again.

"Is that it, Annie? You done? Case for the prosecution closed, is it?"

"Sorry, Rob. I didn't mean to... it all came out in a bit of a rush, didn't it? It's just... it's been bothering me for weeks now, so...."

"Okay. It's crazy. *You're* being crazy, but I can explain easily enough. Don't really see why I should, but I will. Okay?"

She nodded.

"The boxers. That was Laura. She saw my Y-fronts drying one day and said, '*Daaaad!* Oh my God! Y-fronts. What the *hell?* Nobody under like, ninety, wears Y-fronts anymore. Get some boxers for god's sake.'"

"Looked to me like it was Y-fronts David Beckham was wearing in that Armani advert,' I said to her."

"And she said, 'Don't quite know how to break this to you gently, dad, but you are so *not* David Beckham. And those things… well Marks and Sparks didn't sell Armani last time I looked.'"

"What could I say? Next thing, she'd bought me three pairs of silk boxers for my birthday, red, black and the cream with the red hearts for a laugh. You *must* remember that, after all you were there when I opened them. And she said, 'Just don't, like, model them for me dad.' Remember?"

"Yes, you're right, she did. How could I possibly forget something like that? And yes, I remember her saying that now. Or something like that anyway."

"Yes she did. And I did wear them, to please her *and* wound her up by modelling them for her one morning. The cream pair with the hearts. Never seen her so embarrassed. But you know what? I discovered I really liked them, liked the way they felt, and they *do* look way better than Y-fronts, so I bought myself some more and I've been wearing them ever since. The weight loss? Well that's down to Laura as well. When she was explaining to me that I didn't have Beckham's body, she didn't put it *quite* like that."

"No, I don't suppose she did."

"What she *actually* said was, I'm only forty-two and I had a flabby core, soft cheeks and man boobs. Once I'd worked out exactly what she meant, I took a long look in the mirror and decided she was right. So I cut out the biscuits and sweets, started walking the short journeys instead of driving, walking upstairs at work instead of using the lift, those sorts of things. It's not like I've joined a gym and go weight training six times a week, is it?"

He took his time drying his hands and face before he looked at her again.

"What was the other thing? Oh yes, the aftershave. Well, can't blame Laura for that one, can I? *That* was your Mother. Remember she bought me some for my birthday? The Aramis? Remember you made some comment to her at the time? About how it was a bit of a personal present to be buying for her son-in-law."

"Well it was! Sometimes I think she fancies you, old as she is. The way she looks at you sometimes – and touches you. When it's not really necessary."

"Hmmm. Don't know if I dare say it, but I've got news for you, Annie."

"No! She *hasn't!* Has she?"

"She's certainly tried. Remember the party we had last New Year's Eve? All of us pissed, everybody dancing with everybody else. She grabbed me for a dance just after I'd had one with you. You can imagine the aroused state I was in by then. Because of that, I tried to hold her away from me but she wasn't having any of it. Got in real close and then smiled. Told me she wished we were somewhere private so she could see what it was all about rather than just feel it. And then spent the next ten minutes grinding herself against it. And at midnight, when she kissed me? Got her tongue all the way in before I could pull away. Told me I was no fun at all."

"My mother? The bloody *cow*! I *knew* it. I did. Her and all those inappropriate touches she gives you. I'll bloody kill her next time I see her!"

"You'll do no such thing, Annie," he said. "It's never happened since. Mainly because I never let myself be alone with her, or hadn't you noticed?"

"No I hadn't."

"And it isn't going to either. One thing though, you called her old but she's only fifty six. That's no age these days. And she does keep herself in shape, her yoga, aerobics and whatnot. Got a good body for her age. And you were right about the aftershave. It *was* personal. Said she wanted to smell it on me first time I wore it."

Annie shook her head violently, as if to settle her thoughts into a different shape, a different place.

39

"And despite her comment, I thought, bloody hell, I haven't used aftershave since you and me were going out, so I thought I'd try it again. And I liked it. So yes, I use it every day but it doesn't mean that women throw themselves at me in the street. That sort of stuff only happens in adverts, or movies, and I can tell you, the women at work aren't dropping their knickers for me all over the place. *Okay?*"

He expected some response to all that, but not the one he got.

"But you don't just shave your face these days. What's that all about?"

"*Whaat?*"

"You shave down there," she said, nodding towards his boxers. "You've started shaving your... your..."

"Genitals?"

"Well, yes, if you want to put it like that."

"Is there any other way to put it? Penis and testicles? Bit formal that, for us. You are allowed to say cock and balls, Annie, you're not seven years old anymore and you've have handled them a bit over the years."

"Don't be disgusting! And you do shave them, it's weird."

"No, *you* find it weird, not the same thing at all. So tell me, when did you first notice?"

"I dunno," she said, "about six months ago, I suppose."

"Right after my hernia op."

"Yes." She shifted her feet and leaned against the doorway. But kept her arms folded across her breasts. Still with the hard nipples, he thought.

"So why the hell didn't you just ask me, say something, at the time? When you first noticed? You knew I'd been shaved for the op, why didn't you just ask when you saw I carried on doing it? Why store everything up 'til it becomes a real problem for you... and me?"

He stepped over to her and put his hands on her upper arms.

"Like I said, they shaved me for the op, Annie. Remember? And you know what? Afterwards I sort of liked the feel of it, the freedom, whatever, so I kept doing it. Didn't like the full plucked chicken they gave me, but I've kept on doing the rest. Especially since Laura got me the silk boxers. Why? Because it feels absolutely *terrific*, that's why." He grinned. "And there's a bonus as well. It looks a bit longer plus you don't have to pick the hairs out of your teeth."

"Do you have to be *so* bloody crude?"

"Hey, I'm just trying to lighten the mood a little. Because I'm finding it difficult to take all this seriously."

He kissed her on the cheek. And noticed that she flushed. So he kissed her again. Then kissed her neck. Then her bare shoulder. She grabbed his face and kissed him full on the mouth. Put her tongue in his mouth. He could feel his erection growing.

He kissed her back and thumbed her nipples. She kissed him harder, put both hands on his buttocks and pulled him to her. He lifted the t-shirt, reached down and found she was aroused and ready.

They made love up against the bathroom wall, a teenage-style 'knee-trembler' that left them both breathless and sweating. And her crying.

He took her hand, led her though to the bedroom and pulled her onto the bed. They made love again, slowly, intensely, desperately, until she came again. Then she moved him away, straddled him and slid him inside her.

"Sorry," she said….

He put a finger on her lips. "No, don't, it's okay, I…"

"No, I'm really sorry. I am. It's just that, along with the other stuff that's been in my head, the sex hasn't been the same. Not like this. That, and the bathroom. It was fantastic. The passion's just not there like that anymore. I think hearing about what my mother did, imagining you and her together, having sex, must've turned me on in some weird way."

"Annie, honey, we've been married for almost twenty years. The passion, the sort of real passion you're talking about, like we've just experienced, it goes after a while with *everybody*. It doesn't mean there's anything wrong with *us*, we're just human, after all. The sex just becomes *different,* that's all. And it's still good with us, normally. You know it is."

"Yes. Yes it is. But nothing like just now. And yes, I know, it can't always be, but, it's just… *aaaah,* I don't know, don't listen to me, it's just my own insecurities flying around here. I don't really doubt you, course I don't, I doubt myself. It's the giving up my job…"

"Get another. I've told you. Get into work again before Laura goes off to Uni. You're well qualified and got years of experience behind you. You should do it."

"Yes, I know," she said. "And I will. But it's not just that. It's the approaching forty thing. I sailed through thirty, despite what everybody says about *that* barrier, but getting closer to forty really is bugging me. Forty means I'm *really* starting to get old."

She shook her head and laughed.

"*And* it's having a seventeen-year-old beauty who attracts them like flies. It's all affecting me I guess, remembering myself at the same age, the thrills, the emotions, everything sharp, intense. And I know it can't ever be the same way again, but when I look at myself…"

"Hey. Annie. I love you just the way you are. We've grown up together so you're the same to me now as you always were. Even if you are thirty-eight. And I've already passed forty, don't forget. I'm further along the road than you are and I always will be. You'll always be the young one in the partnership so don't forget that when you're giving yourself a hard time about your age."

She leaned forward and kissed him on the forehead. Then the nose. Then a quick peck on the lips.

"You're too sweet, you are. And like a lot of men, you just look better as you get older, 'specially since Laura took you in hand. Nothing's gone south on you yet. Not like me after the two kids…"

He shook his head and smiled.

"But I don't see that. Don't you understand? You look gorgeous to me. I just feel you, see you, the same as I always have done. My Annie. The gorgeous girl I first saw in the club that night. All mini skirt and false eyelashes. Tasty then, tasty now. Although you could join me in the shaving. Make at least one part of you look twenty years younger, you're so concerned about your body."

But said it with a grin. And laughed when she grinned as well and smacked him on the chest. He moved out from under and cuddled into her.

"Listen, why don't we go out tonight and celebrate. Milano's? Lots of pasta and red wine? Freddy's okay when Laura's here. How about it, yeah?"

"Yes," she said, kissing his chest. "That would be lovely. Really lovely. We can take a taxi so both of us can have a proper drink. Now you better get moving, or you're going to be very late."

He kissed her again, rolled out of bed and had his second shower of the morning. He grabbed a quick coffee in the kitchen while he packed his brief case and put his jacket on. She straightened his tie and gave him a last, long, lingering kiss before he went to the door.

"Sorry," she said again. "Ignore me, I'm just being pre-menopausal."

"Shut up. Love you," he said.

"Love you too. And not *too* much pasta and wine for you tonight though because I'll be expecting a replay of this morning."

He squeezed her buttocks and walked out of the front door. He laid his jacket and brief case on the back seat of the Audi, plugged in his mobile and pulled out of the drive. He drove to end of street, turned right and was out of sight of the house.

He punched in the office number on speed dial. After a couple of rings he heard a familiar voice.

"*Hello!* This is late for you. Are you on your way in now?"

"She knows."

LOVE IS A STOPPED TRAIN

Less than two minutes out from Berlin, the Frankfurt Express came to a sudden, juddering, unexplained stop.

The majority of the passengers being German, however, there was no more reaction than a few raised eyebrows and gentle shakes of the head. Fifteen minutes passed in relative silence before an announcement was made apologising for the delay. In clear and precise terms it was explained that a body of a man, presumed to have been a passenger, had been found next to the track and that the authorities had been informed.

Also, the violent braking had been caused by a door in a first-class carriage having been opened. Something which, without the correct electronic key, was not possible on a German high-speed inter-city express train. The surprise and disapproval were evident in the announcer's voice.

Further information would be given as and when it became available, he added. The passengers seemed reassured by that, settled back in their seats and continued the conversations that had been so rudely interrupted.

Ten minutes later, a curious passenger would have been able to see the flashing blue lights of Police vehicles a few hundred yards down the line. After a brief and, it must be said, cursory examination of the damage to the clothes and body, the police constables first on the scene determined that the man had died falling from the train. Paramedics were called and, as the regulations demanded, a doctor was requested to attend.

It took less than twenty minutes for the doctor to arrive and, judging by the immaculate way he was dressed, he had been collected from a restaurant or private party. Wearing clothing totally unsuitable for kneeling next to a railway line and examining a dead body. He stared at the policemen with his hands spread wide, palms up in silent question.

One of the constables quickly understood and fetched a large waterproof jacket from the van and spread it on the ground for him. It took him less than thirty seconds before he stood up, dusted off his trousers and, his face diffused with anger, he began castigating the policemen.

Calling them idiots, morons and worse, he instructed them to call a murder squad Inspector and at least twenty more policemen. In answer to their surprised and puzzled faces, he pointed out the four stab wounds that had been partially obscured by the other damage to the corpse. But only partially.

Patiently, but firmly, he explained that it was not an accident and not suicide. Not unless they thought the man was acrobatic enough to stab himself in the back as he was falling from a train travelling at almost 70 miles an hour. Perhaps a contortionist he said sarcastically? Added that he hoped this experience would teach them to make a much more thorough initial examination in future. They all nodded, embarrassed. Finally, he instructed them not to touch the body again until the Inspector arrived.

In the end it was a Senior Chief Inspector who appeared having been at a meeting not far from the scene. He took charge until a humble Inspector could be made available. Using the same spread jacket, he knelt and examined the body, nodding as the doctor pointed out the stab wounds. He then was able to identify the man because both passport and driving licence had been carefully zipped into the inside pockets of his suit jacket.

Herr Friedrich von Hartmann. Occupation: banker. Address in Frankfurt. But not just any banker it turned out. The business card in his wallet stated that he was the chairman of a private investment bank in Frankfurt and a senior advisor to the *Bundesministerium der Finanzen* - the Federal Ministry of Finance.

The Chief Inspector took out his phone and Googled Herr Hartman whereupon he discovered that the banker was a close personal friend of the Finance Minister himself. He absorbed this information and thought about the resultant pressure it would bring - political, the worst kind for any policeman.

He showed the card and 'phone to the doctor who raised his eyebrows and wished the Chief Inspector the very best of luck. Sincerely.

"You will need it with those bastards," the doctor said. "Watch your back my friend."

Given this information, he decided this could not be delegated to an Inspector. Whoever turned up would have to work as his assistant because they could not be expected to deal with senior government officials and politicians. Or, indeed, the Police President himself.

Still pondering on the problems that lay ahead, he ordered eight policemen up the track to the train, four either side, to make sure no-one tried to get off.

Within minutes, more vans arrived and deposited two dozen police officers, including two sergeants. Most of the constables had never been in the presence of a Senior Chief Inspector before and they stood stiffly to attention, thumbs down the seams of their trousers. He looked them all over and then explained that every metre from where the body lay to the front of the train, inside and out, was a crime scene and they were to begin a fingertip search.

While sixteen of them began searching, two were instructed to detain all the train attendants to determine which of their keys had been used to open the door. Once that was known, she or he was to be arrested. The other four, the most experienced present, were sent to deal with the passengers.

Five minutes later, a young woman Inspector arrived on a BMW motorbike. She climbed off, removed her helmet, saluted and introduced herself. No make-up or jewellery he noticed, and he took in her heavy-duty jacket and trousers and sturdy boots. He nodded in silent approval.

"Good afternoon, Inspector Lange. I know your name and reputation, but I don't think we've ever met, have we?"

"No, sir, although I did attend your lecture earlier this year on successful interrogation techniques."

He nodded. "And did you agree with my main argument that violent methods do not produce the required results?"

"I did, sir, and I'm surprised your methods have not been adopted across the force. I think your superiors are being very short-sighted."

"Perhaps so," he said with a smile. "But you must remember Inspector that the highest rank doesn't equate to the highest intelligence. There is no direct connection."

She nodded and stifled a laugh. "But my reputation? What do you mean?"

"I know of your exemplary record," he said, "but I was particularly referring to the fact that they call you Die Eiserne Frau, yes?"

"The Iron Woman. Yes, they do… but never to my face. I quite like it sir, because in order to survive and prosper in the Berlin police, I have had to be stronger, harder, more resilient than the men. It wasn't easy, and it took some time, but they don't patronise me any longer. They know exactly what I will tolerate, and they don't cross my lines."

I just bet they don't, he thought.

"And I understand your competence is beyond question also," he said. "Which you will need in this case. Have you ever worked on a murder inquiry?"

Her eyes widened in surprise. "Yes, I have, although only as a junior member of a team. But murder? I was told that this was an accidental death."

"An initial mistake was made," he said and then explained exactly who the victim was and the political pressure that would inevitably be applied. She nodded her understanding.

"That is why I will deal with the politicians and the most senior officers," he said, "leaving you free to command the investigation. The people involved at their level wouldn't even speak to an Inspector, especially when that Inspector is female."

"In that case, sir, would it be possible for me to bring in my best sergeant, Karl Müller? He is extremely competent, and I trust him completely."

The Chief Inspector nodded. "You will find that during an investigation with these possible implications, no reasonable request will be refused. I trust you understand the power you have in this case and will use it with intelligence and good judgement. Just e-mail me your request for Müller and I will authorise it. No need for lengthy information," he said. "A simple request will do."

She expressed her gratitude and then said, "If I may make a suggestion, sir?"

He nodded, the said, "You should understand, Inspector, that this investigation is already in your hands. You don't need my permission for any proposals."

He paused. "But I am interested. What is it?"

"We need more constables," she said. "Given the time it would have taken the train to come to a halt, I think we should also search back from the body. The weapon might well have been thrown out with it."

He nodded again. Sensible woman, he thought. And indeed competent. "Agreed," he said. "Make the call, Inspector and use my name only if you have any difficulties."

She thanked him again and turned to speak to the sergeants, relaxing slightly when she realised that she knew one of them. Although not as good as Karl, she had worked with him before, and since they respected each other's skills and capabilities, she was confident there would be no stupid gender issues.

* * * * *

As an ambulance carried the body away, four officers boarded the train and began slowly walking through the compartments, two from the front, two from the rear, demanding identification and questioning the passengers. Recording everything in notebooks.

A further announcement was then made informing everyone that they must remain in their seats because the train was now a crime scene. Anyone who ignored this instruction would be arrested and charged with obstructing the police.

They were also informed that the train would make an unscheduled stop at Charlottenburg station and would remain there until every passenger had been questioned. Another train would then be brought up to allow anyone not detained to continue their journey to Frankfurt.

In typical German fashion, the announcement was part apology, part direct instruction and brought no noticeable reaction from the passengers. Apart, that is, from a party of four drunken Englishmen wearing football shirts, who were playing dominos amongst a mess of more than a dozen empty beer cans. With unopened ones close at hand.

They were vocal in their objections booing and jeering until they realised that no-one else in the carriage was paying them any attention. No-one had even lifted their head, never mind joined in with their protest. So they laughed, shrugged their shoulders, opened fresh cans and noisily carried on with their game.

They then studiously ignored the two police officers who approached them demanding to see their identification. Until one of the officers, irritated by these drunken Englishmen, unhooked his baton and with a quick left-right flick of the wrist, cleared most of the dominos from the table.

Before they could object, he laid the baton firmly on the shoulder of the most vocal of the four and applied gentle but firm pressure. At the same time, his colleague produced a pair of handcuffs and dangled them in front of the men's faces. Passports were then quickly handed over and all questions politely, if grudgingly, answered.

The nearby passengers quietly smiled and nodded their approval. They had always known what the outcome would be, but they were curious to see whether the Englishmen would try to assert themselves.

Meanwhile, in a first-class carriage, the widow Hartmann continues reading her book, as yet unaware that she is, officially, a widow. Although her quiet, almost contented smile suggests that when delivered, the news will come as no surprise to her at all.

COITUS INTERRUPTUS

His girlfriend grunted and pushed Grant away. It was his day off and they were in his bed in the middle of the afternoon.

"Sorry," he said turning his face to hers on the pillow. "Was I too rough?"

"No! God, no. It was bloody wonderful. And very different coming from you. No, it's just the way you were lying against me there, my leg and arm have gone to sleep. Aaaaaaaaahhh! I've got pins and needles now."

She lifted her arm and leg off the bed and started giggling. Grant slowly massaged her thigh and calf.

"You go any higher up there and we'll have to do all that pre-cramp stuff again," she said, still giggling.

"Like before you mean."

"Mmmmmm," she said as his hand slid up her inner thigh. "Just like before… like that, would be absolutely fine… but, seriously, where did that come from all of a sudden?"

She dropped her leg, trapping his hand between her thighs.

"You liked it then?"

"I should say."

"But I seem to remember you telling me once that you didn't like violence. Have you changed your mind now?"

She shifted against him as he freed his hand and slid an arm along the pillow behind her head. So, it's talk not action now he thought. Hey ho. But he still slid his free hand back down onto her thigh. Just in case.

"Violence I don't like, you're right. But that wasn't violent. That was alive and a wee bit rough and I liked it. Very much so," she said biting his shoulder. "It's... ex... ci... ting!" she murmured, nipping him with her teeth on every syllable.

"But you haven't answered me, where did it come from? Or should I say who's been turning you on?"

"Why should anybody else be turning me on?" he asked. "Are you saying I'm usually boring in bed, is that it?"

"No, not boring at all, David. You're gentle, considerate, you take your time, and I like that. It's just that sometimes I like... well... *not* so considerate. And when it's so different, it usually means someone's been turning somebody on. Or just maybe getting them frustrated in some other way."

"That's more like it," he said smiling. "It's all my anger and frustration at bloody Davidson coming out now, the bastard. He'd be absolutely raging if he knew you were getting the hidden benefits."

"DCI Davidson?" she said, "but that man is a total sweetheart."

"You're winding me up now," he said. "A total sweetheart? Davidson? You *must* be joking. I've heard him called a lot of things but never that. He's an arrogant, callous, bullying, self-centered, self-serving, amoral, narcissistic shit. And that's just for starters. Give me a few minutes and I'll come up with a few more choice adjectives."

"He's never any of that with me. Or patronising, *And* he doesn't use foul and abusive language either."

"Jesus! Anything else you want to have a go at me for?"

"Seriously, David, you won't find a woman solicitor or barrister who has a bad word to say about him. He's so very different from most men - most policemen, especially."

"What? How do you mean? Because I just don't get it."

"You wouldn't. You're a man. What it is, he treats all us women of the law as capable professionals with skills and abilities that are both useful and valuable. *And* he always notices and compliments me on what I'm wearing or if I've had my hair cut, which is more than I can say for some so-called observant policemen of this parish. That's a deadly combination in any man. Respect as a person, as a lawyer and recognition as an attractive woman? Makes him an absolute sweetheart in my book."

"But all that hair and clothes stuff, I thought you'd regard that as sexist... being regarded as a sex object I mean. Objectivising you."

"God, your parents have a lot to answer for, the understanding you've got of women. I've no problem being objectivised *as well*, it's when it's the *only* thing, I take exception. A lot of women want to be respected *and* fancied a bit, it's..."

"But It's just a bloody device with that bastard, he's clever enough to string you lot..."

"Really? *'You lot?'* Well... thank you very much for that, David. But you're quite wrong. He's too consistent with it. If it was just a technique he applied, it would slip sometimes, his real attitudes would show through. Because he's not *smooth* with it. And he's like it with all the women, not just the so-called attractive ones."

"Which category do you come in, then?"

"You cheeky bugger," she said, kneeing him sharply in the thigh. "Just for that you can get your own bloody drink." She slid out of the bed and walked, naked, into the kitchen.

55

Watching her, David Grant wondered, yet again, how he'd been so lucky. Why had this stunning woman chosen him? Because chosen was how it had been. He'd seen her around the Courts for months, found her almost unbearably attractive but never dared speak to her. He'd eventually discovered she was two years younger than him, but in every way except physical appearance she seemed older and much more mature. He thought she was way out of his league. She was a barrister, after all, and there he was, just a humble detective sergeant. Okay, with a law degree, but a mere 2:2 from Manchester, provincial red brick to her Oxbridge bluestocking First.

Then she'd prosecuted a high-profile case of his and for three months he had every opportunity to get closer to her. And still he couldn't bring himself to ask her out. In the end, she asked him. Once the case had ended in a win for her - and him - she asked him if he fancied a celebratory drink. Astonished, he somehow managed to say yes. A few drinks and a meal later, she took him to bed that first night. And every time since.

Now, he watched her body move again as she walked back carrying a huge glass of white wine and climbed into bed beside him.

"Did you not get me my lager, then?" he asked as she took a first generous mouthful.

"I told you, you could get your own after that little crack. And I meant it. You'll learn, David. Or you'll suffer."

"You're worse than bloody Davidson," he said as he went to the fridge for a cold bottle.

"What's the matter, darling," she called. "Bruised your delicate male ego, did I, complimenting another man? Hinting there might just be a valid opinion of somebody other than the male one?"

Despite himself, he smiled as he heard the laugh in her voice. No other woman he'd known could be so right all the bloody time without being obnoxious with it. He opened the fridge, took a bottle out and uncapped it.

"D'you want a couple of these chocolate eclairs as well?"

"Yes, please! If you're sure you can be bothered to bring me some, that is."

"Of course, my sweet. After all, I'm not a man to hold grudges... even if I'm not right up there with DCI Davidson."

He put two eclairs and his bottle of lager on a tray and walked back into the bedroom.

"Wooooh, David. If all waiters wore that uniform, you'd never get a table in the whole of London... Oh look! it's moving! David, what does *that* mean?"

"Means It's getting cold. That's just it shivering," he said, not daring to laugh in case he dropped the tray.

"But I thought they got smaller when they got cold. You know, like when you go in the sea. But I swear It's getting bigger."

"Shut up, you. And move over," he said, putting the tray on the bedside table. "Food and drink first."

"Incurable romantic, you are. You mean to say you'd take eclairs and lager before me? I see."

"No, not before. In between I should've said."

"What? You mean there's more to come? Good oh." she said, taking a bite of an eclair and licking her fingers.

"Play your cards right, there could be," he said, propping himself up beside her.

"Tell me something David," she said when they were comfortable. "Would you ever have asked me out if I hadn't invited you for a drink that day?"

"Probably not."

"Why not? You clearly fancied me."

"Yes, of course I did, but I didn't think you fancied me at all."

"Because…?"

"Well, there you were, tall, beautiful, capable, with that private girl's school and Oxbridge confidence, I didn't think you even saw me apart from just this prole copper who gave evidence every now and then."

"Ooh, no," she laughed, "you couldn't be more wrong. You were a very bright, good looking '*prole copper*', as you put it, and all we women thought you had the best bum on any man who came to the courts. And we reckoned you filled your boxers pretty well, too."

"God, you women. And you accuse me of being sexist at times."

"What? Are we any different from men? You trying to tell me you lot don't examine and speculate about every attractive woman's body? So why can't we women? And anyway," she said, sliding her hand down the bed and taking him in her hand, "we were quite right about the boxers. *Very* impressive this is," she said, giving him a little squeeze.

"Enough of that," he said. "I need food and drink and a little time to recover."

* * * * *

"So, tell me about Davidson," she said when they'd both finished eating. "What's he been doing to you now? And don't give me that look, David. You've mentioned him three times in the last half an hour - when your mind should have been on other things - so he's obviously done *something.*"

"Yes. He has. But it's not me he's done it to. Not really. He just treats me the same way he treats every other policeman, with a mixture of contempt, sarcasm, piss-taking and occasional faint praise. *Very* faint praise. There's only two things save him. The fact that he's bloody good at what he does, he gets results, and he treats us all the same, from the Chief Constable to the newest probationer."

"I don't..."

"No. Let me finish. Just let me dump this on you. I've been dying to tell somebody and I daren't talk to anyone on the job..."

She laughed. "What do you call this then?"

As she said it, she noticed some cream filling from the éclair had dropped onto her breast and she lifted her fingers to remove it. But then paused and cupped her breasts in her hands instead. She half turned and offered them to him.

"Want to clean this last piece of cream off me?"

"Get your mind above the waist, you. You're positively pornographic."

"Well, my mind is, at least. And what I'm offering to you are well above the waist. They don't sag an inch. And as for pornographic? Can eating cream from your girlfriend's breast, in private, without any cameras around, be defined as *'pornographic'* under the terms of the Act? Good argument in that one... Oh well," she said, when she realised he wasn't going to make a move towards her. "I'll do it myself."

Looking directly at him and smiling, she scooped the cream off her breast and licked her fingers clean.

"You're wicked, you know that? And you know what I meant. There's way too many agendas around for me to start confiding in anyone at the station. It would just give them ammunition to use against me. In that job, they'd damage me for life they could. And stop sucking your bloody fingers like that, woman, I can't concentrate."

Grant thought about the enemies his DCI had made in the Force and what would happen to him if Davidson ever found out he'd voiced his doubts to any of them. A transfer to Traffic would be the least of his worries.

"No. It's not me, It's the bloody case." She raised her eyebrows at him. "The Collins case. The attempted murder. Remember? Yeah, thought you would. It's more than he does, remember it's a case, I mean. Because he's not doing any proper police work at all."

"You're losing me, David," she said, wiping her fingers on the duvet.

"You should worry. I'm totally lost and I'm working with him. Because he's done no detecting, no evidence gathering, and no interviewing. There's no case notes at all. Can you believe that? Not one entry in a notebook, not even any scribbles on paper. He destroys all that every day. Everything. *And* he's using private investigators, civilians, to do his legwork. All that with Blair standing over his shoulder. Oh yeah, he's well on the case," he said when he saw her look of surprise. "And still he's not done one bloody thing we normally do on any case, never mind one like this."

"I don't understand," she said. "How does he expect to solve it then?"

"That's just it, he doesn't." He shook his head and took a swig of his lager.

"You're not making any sense, David. What are you talking about? When it first happened, you talked about nothing else for a week. I thought something had happened because you've hardly mentioned it at all this week. But you've still been busy, you and Davidson. You must've been, because I've hardly seen you. What have you been busy doing if not trying to solve the case?"

"Killing people," he said, staring at the ceiling.

"Oh, David, come on."

She laughed and turned on her side to look at him. But when she saw his face, she realised he wasn't being flippant. Although she'd only known him for six months, she already knew when he was being serious. But how on earth could he be serious about something like that?

"Hey," she said, poking him gently in the ribs. "Talk to me. Tell me what you meant. Killing people? That's a hell of a thing to say."

"That's because It *is* a hell of thing. And it's happening. Seriously now. He's killing people, Detective Chief Inspector Davidson is. Or getting people killed, to be more precise. That's what I said and that's what I meant. I wasn't joking, being ironic or sarcastic, any of those things. I'm talking facts. Factual. Want another little fact? I'm helping him. Actively by going with him on some of his little sadistic visits, and passively by not saying anything up the line. Aiding and abetting that's called. With knowledge aforethought. Malice aforethought even. You should bloody know, *Madame* barrister."

61

She sat up beside him, resting back against the headboard. He had her attention now. Her friends all said he was too serious for her but she knew his seriousness had its limits. He had a lighter side to him, especially when they were on their own, but he still had that absolute sense of right and wrong she'd often noticed in new policemen.

It usually wore off by the time they became sergeants, but David was different. He hadn't become cynical, not yet, and she found she liked him the more for it. His relationship with Davidson was complex, especially because David was a graduate, and it was something she normally left well alone. But this was too intriguing.

"Explain," she said softly. "Tell me."

"Remember I told you Collins practically killed that guy, in front of witnesses, and we couldn't believe it when people told us it was him? Then we found out the guy had some sort of connection with Doyle's daughter and *then* found out Collins was having an affair with her?"

She nodded and snuggled into him, her arm across his chest and her head on his shoulder. Then she felt the way his heart was beating and suddenly realised just how much all this meant to him.

"The investigation started as normal. Textbook procedure, talking to as many people we could find, all that basic stuff. We'd been given the name Collins in a phone call we got, that's how we knew what had happened, but we didn't think *Davey* Collins. Why would we? Not his style at all. He's the Coyle family enforcer for god's sake and the guy he attacked, Watson, wasn't connected at all.   Just an ordinary youngster. We interviewed people in the bar just after it happened and got the usual. Three wise monkeys. *"What, officer? No, only been here five minutes. Ambulance? Always see them round here. Collins? Never heard of no Collins."*

Neither of us believed them of course but what can you do? You need one to break ranks and round there, in that pub, they wouldn't dare. More than their life's worth."

"So how did you get the connection with Collins if nobody spoke up?"

"Not in the pub I said. But afterwards, we went to the hospital to talk to the family. There was some family row going on, I think. Davidson pushed a bit and the father lost it. He gave us Collins as well. But *Davey* Collins this time. And that we could *not* believe. You couldn't, nobody could. We thought it was a wind up. But he was insistent. Collins did it he said. His wife and son tried to shut him up, but he said it again before they finally managed to stop him. The younger brother seemed to know something about what was going on, even though he's only ten, but he wouldn't say a bloody word to us. They train them young and they train them well round those parts."

"Don't tell me, he doesn't like policemen."

"Him and a few million others. And when we spoke to Watson, he'd never seen the guy before in his life of course. Hadn't a clue what it was all about. Then we started thinking and doing things properly, timelines and such. And guess what? The phone call we received came in at least ten minutes *before* Collins attacked the guy. So we thought some more. How did Watson's family know who it was so quickly? We talked to the staff and a guy, we don't know who, was seen talking to the family about an hour before we got there. And we think Collins found out about it."

"But that's all proper police procedure, you said he'd…"

"Yes, you're right, it is. But since then, nothing. He's done absolutely nothing except put Collins under more and more pressure."

She wanted to say there was nothing unusual about policemen putting pressure on criminals but quickly decided this was not the time.

"He went to see Collins himself, at his snooker club, in front of witnesses for god's sake, the sort of witnesses they get in there! Let him know he knew what he'd done. Virtually told him that Doyle's sons had set him up, were out to get him. And that was after he'd taken Collins's mother out for a drink…"

"His mother? What on earth…"

"Apparently they grew up in the same area, next street or something, known her since he was a boy. Anyway, he took her out for a few drinks, let her know he knew what Collins had done and told her about Doyle's boys setting him up for it. Tried to get her to talk to Collins."

"And he's close to his mother still, Collins?"

"Very. She brought him up herself after his father walked out. And he told her that her son was out of his depth for the first time, there was nothing he could do about it, that she might not have a son too much longer."

"*Jesus!*"

"He could've invoked him as well, for all I know, he was so pissed when we picked him up. And stood there in the centre of bloody town, in broad daylight while he poured her into a taxi. Unbelievable."

"How do you not know what was said, if you were there."

"That's just it," Grant said. "I wasn't, either time. No witness, no corroboration. Just his word about what happened."

"What? But he's usually so punctilious about that sort of thing. Does it by the book."

"Don't I know it. But not on those two occasions. Plenty of civilian witnesses, but no policemen. Didn't even tell me he was going to do it, either. Just told me what had happened, what he *says* happened, afterwards."

"Have you checked his notebook, his diary?"

"I'm ahead of you for once. Yes I did and no, there's no record, no mention, of either meeting."

"Why's he..."

"Wait. Wait. The next thing, he went to see Collins's girlfriend - Doyle's daughter. Doyle's just about old enough twenty-year-old daughter. But took me this time though. Not to get anything from her, you understand, just to frighten her. Just to scare the bloody life out of her, in fact. Bring the other side of her boyfriend into her life as Davidson put it. And to flush Collins out and let him know we knew he was screwing her."

"How on earth did he manage that?"

"Hung around afterwards in the car, about fifty feet from the front door."

"That would do it."

"You haven't heard the best. The bastard also went and second-guessed Collins by dropping in to have a drink with a bunch of his old mates, upright citizens all of them. Not a speeding or parking ticket amongst them. *That* happened just a few days before Collins did the same thing himself for the first time in about ten years. And don't ask me how Davidson worked *that* one out because I haven't got a clue. Then he made sure Collins was breathalysed when he came out. He was well over the limit, so the uniforms brought him into the station. Davidson pissed him about for half an hour or so then let him go. Actually had the station sergeant pull the breathalyser. Nothing in the book."

"I see what you mean about pressure."

"That's nothing. There he is Collins, just done a civilian, a young boy, for the first time ever and totally out of character whatever else you say about him, and he must be worried shitless that Doyle'll find out he's screwing his daughter, wondering when the fuck the two boys are going to make their move and he's got this sadistic bastard tracking him all over the city. Family, his wife, secret girlfriends and everything."

"Then to cap it all - and I suspect Davidson had a hand in this as well though I can't prove it - his wife, wife of twenty-five years, throws him out. Must've found out about his girlfriend – although not who she actually is. He's got no breathing space anywhere. That's what I call pressure."

"Absolutely," she said. "I bet he can't wait for New Year's Eve to come round."

"For Christ's sake, this is no joke! Collins is a maniac. And he's vanished. Completely. Last time we saw him was at his girlfriend's. Three weeks ago his world was normal, now he hasn't bloody got one. The only way he'll react to that sort of pressure is to kill somebody."

"David, David. Please don't exaggerate. Perhaps he isn't following the book on this one. It happens. You know that better than I do. But he hasn't broken any law that I know of. I thought he had, the way you were talking. What's so bad?"

He slowly shook his head. Then turned to look at her.

"You've not been listening to me," he said, speaking very quietly. And there's me thinking your mind always worked like it does when you're in Court. Lighting a fire under him, was how he put it. He told me he's pushing Collins until he kills whoever grassed on hm, then the Doyle boys - and whoever else happens to get in the way - and then we'll pick him up for it."

"You're not..."

"Oh, but I am. He's pushing him and following him so we can catch him post facto. Except the facto is already bloody post, because he already has."

"What?"

"Collins has already killed one that we're sure of. That sneaky little bastard called Charlie Watkins. We're pretty sure he's the one called us about the incident at the pub *and* told Watson's family. He was found hanging from a chain in a scrapyard the other morning. With the guard dogs dead nearby. His nose and both his arms and legs had been broken before he was hung, but it was the hanging that killed him. So Collins wanted information and Watkins wasn't the sort of man who could resist that kind of treatment. And guess who owns the scrapyard - where there was no sign of a break in, by the way? A close friend of Collins, that's who. Gave him the keys, we're sure of it - but can't prove it of course.

"But that's just circumstantial. Why are you so sure it actually was Collins?"

"Because we've *actually* got evidence, witnesses who put him at the scene... well his car anyway. We've got shoe prints we're sure we could match to his shoes and we've even got his prints on a crowbar that's got traces of Watkins' blood and bone on it."

"Well that's evidence enough to build a good case," she said. "The crowbar's safely in the evidence lock-up..."

"You'd think. Oh it's safely locked up alright, just not where it should be. He's got it in the combination cupboard in his office."

She stared at him, astonished. "*Whaat?* Don't tell me he didn't even book it in at all...."

"Got it in one," he said.

"But that's unbelievable. Have you *said* anything to him?"

"Of course. He just laughs, tells me not to get my knickers in a twist. Happened all the time back when he was a constable."

"Christ almighty!"

"Yes. Although I somehow don't think he'd approve. So... We've got all that and do we pick him up? Do we hell. We don't even try to find where he's gone to ground. Your adorable *Mister* Davidson's done sod all about it except to put more and more pressure on him. And you know what Davidson's like, it's not like he's got an off switch. More importantly, neither has Collins, he's still out there going after people. And Davidson's just pushing him harder and harder. We've even got a fair idea who else he's after and why he's doing it. More than a fair idea. But have we warned them? Not at all. So there you have it. What's your considered view on that little lot, Counsellor?"

She moved away from him and drew her knees up to her chin. "I Don't think you should have told me all of that, David," she said quietly. "Don't tell me any more."

He turned to face her. Angry now.

"Oh what? So you don't see anything wrong in what he's doing then?"

"I didn't say that."

"No. But you didn't say you did, did you?" Almost shouting now. Angry. "Just said not to tell you. Like when you're defending some bastard you know is guilty. But don't ever ask the question because you might just get the wrong answer eh? Could bother your professional conscience knowing a senior policeman did nothing to prevent a capital crime being committed, could it? Not only did nothing about it, actively encouraged it! And I'm a bloody accessory, before, during and after! And you'll defend me, will you? he shouted. "Make a speech in my defense in court?"

"David. Please," she said putting her hand on his chest and stroking him. "I'm a barrister. In a criminal practice. I see and hear all sorts of things I personally disapprove of - so must you. If we reacted to them all the way we probably should, we'd never get anything done. And anyway, just let me be objective for a minute…"

"*Objective!*" Grant was shouting again. "How can you be bloody objective when *I'm* involved? When I'm helping the bastard?"

She ignored his outburst. "Like I said, being objective, and as a barrister, I can easily be that when I need to, if it gets results, if it gets someone like Collins and a few others like him off the streets - and I'm not saying this is me, now, it's just a view, but if it *does* get results, who's to say it's all bad?"

He grabbed her hand and lifted held it away from his chest.

"Oh. Excuse me. And there's me thinking when I joined the force I swore to uphold the law. I seem to remember that. Actually standing up and saying it. Silly of me. Or naive, I suppose. What you don't seem to realise is that if we take your Stalinist approach - end justifying the bloody means - and we use their methods, we end up no better than them. We lose the moral high ground. Just become state-approved thugs. Is that what you want? East fucking Germany? Me as a member of the Stasi?"

"It's not a question of what I want," she said. "Or you, for that matter. Maybe Davidson's simply said, '*bugger the moral high ground*'. If keeping hold of that means these people stay on the street then maybe he's decided to fight them on their own terms and beat them that way. It might not be right but maybe he's decided he'll use his methods instead of the uniform, the power of the state, and the law, to do unto them as they do. It's very Old Testament when you come to think of it."

"Jesus Christ. Is that how you think? Let's base our laws and actions on the Old fucking Testament?"

"I said it wasn't necessarily my..."

"*Bollocks!*" She turned to look at him. Wondering how to change the mood.

"I'm just starting to realise," he said, very calm now. "I really don't know you at all, do I?"

"Oh David, no. No. Not that. Please don't turn this into a you and me thing. Because it isn't."

"But I don't, do I?"

"How could you? We've only known each other for about three months. Of *course* you don't really know me. It takes people an awful lot longer than that. Takes some a lifetime... and even then there's often things they don't know."

"Bullshit! If I know so little about you, with things I care so much about, what are we doing together? What am I doing here?"

"*What?*"

"You heard."

"Okay, if that's the way you feel, I'll leave," she said. "And leave right now."

"Oh no. Don't you move your lady-like arse an inch. I'll go. And don't wait up for me."

He got out of bed and reached for his trousers. She watched him as he struggled into his boxer shorts and then started to pull up his trousers.

"David."

"*What?*"

"What on earth are you doing?" she asked, smiling. Irritating him even more.

"Getting dressed. What does it look like? Then I'm leaving, like I said I would."

"Well… I don't want to be *too* pedantic here, I know how much you hate that, but this is actually *your* bed. Remember? In *your* flat. Not mine. If anyone should be doing any leaving here, by rights it should be me. But then, my ladylike arse is doing exactly what it was told to do. And I can't seem to move. Well… not vertically, anyway. Horizontally though? Well that's a different matter altogether."

He stood by the bed, very still, his back towards her, one foot still in his trousers.

"Tell you what," she said when he didn't turn around. "How about you come back to bed - *your* bed," she said, giggling, "we'll do some of that pre-cramp stuff and we can talk about you and your beloved DCI Davidson some other time. Maybe even immediately afterwards. Pillow talk. How does that sound?"

He turned slowly towards the bed and slipped the trousers off his foot. "Am I that much of an arse?" he asked with a reluctant grin.

"Pretty much," she said, smiling. "But very cute with it. And your arse does look wonderful when you're angry. Come on in here, you."

"I'm not sure I'm in the mood, now," he said. "I feel too much of a prat."

72

"Maybe this will this help?" she said, lifting the duvet and stretching her leg out towards him. She stroked the front of his boxer shorts with her toes as he watched her hand sliding from her breast to her belly and back again.

"Do you know, I think it is. I think he's cured, doctor!" she laughed as he stepped out of his boxer shorts. She stared at him as he straightened up. "All I can say is, if it was cold before, it must be bloody freezing now."

Ten minutes later, their lovemaking was interrupted by the 'phone.

"*Fuck!*" Grant said, freezing above her.

"Yes, please," she said. "Let it ring, and we can."

"I can't. I know, I know, I'm not on duty. But I just can't." Without moving the rest of his body, he snatched up the 'phone. "*What?*"

Davidson's voice mocked him down the line.

"Coitus interruptus is a commonly practiced, if unreliable, form of contraception, Grant. Get her arse out of your hands and get yourself down here. The case won't get solved by itself you know."

"You bastard! How did you..." he started, but the 'phone went dead in his ear. He slammed the receiver down and the phone crashed to the floor.

"What is it, David? What's the matter," she asked as she saw his face redden. "Who *was* that?"

"Who the hell d'you think? It was Davidson, of course. He had the bloody nerve to say the case won't be solved by itself. Bastard! Like we've *got* a bloody case. He must have something new on Collins... but hang on, how did the bastard know where I was? And that you were here. *And* that we were in bed together. I don't..."

73

"He's a policeman, David. And a clever one at that. Doesn't take much to work out, does it? It's your day off, I'm not on any of the court listings so you're bound to be with me. And he does know where you live even if he's never been here. Just relax."

Grant started to ease himself up but she grabbed his arm.

"No, David. Oh no you don't." She wrapped her arms around him and pulled him down to her.

"I've got to go."

"No, you don't. Not just yet. And not like this. You're still in me, nothing's changed as far as I can feel, and another ten minutes isn't going to bring Collins in and anybody back to life, is it? Come on," she said, moving under him. "Let me make you feel nice again, then you can go serve your master."

"Oh God. Will you marry me you wonderful bloody woman?" he said as he closed on her and she moved under him.

"Do you love me?"

"I do, I do. Truly, madly, deeply."

"Correct answer, Sergeant. Okay then. Let's just… yes… finish this and then I'll think about it. It wasn't the most romantic of proposals but I'll… mmmmmm. Oh yes, just like that."

IF MUSIC BE THE FOOD

It was yet another hot Sunday afternoon in that glorious, seemingly never-ending Summer of 1967. At the Serpentine in Hyde Park where everything was dust, the grass yellow and brown and English people were tanned as never before. Girls lay on the grass sunbathing, the more daring of them wearing nothing but bras and knickers. Which got them admiring glances from the young men, lecherous looks from older men and stares of disapproval from their wives. The older generation was not so tolerant or accepting in those days, the "*Summer of Love*" being largely a youth phenomenon.

Following my recent separation, I was just another weekend father who minutes before had handed his son over to his mother. He and I had spent an hour or two in a Serpentine rowing boat where, at the age of eight, he had sat on my lap and 'rowed' with his hands above mine on the oars. I doubt he was fooled for a moment, but he took enormous pride in his achievement.

Afterwards, I walked to the café for coffee and cakes to give myself a much-needed caffeine and sugar boost after the tension and sadness of our latest meeting. As well as the regrets of course, cursing myself for creating the rift and losing the best woman I had ever known. I often wondered why basic intelligence vanished when close personal relationships were involved. Still pondering on my failures, I took my tray and sat outside in the shade, indulging in the age-old pastime of watching the girls go by.

I was still in this dark mood when I suddenly became aware of someone playing a saxophone. And I do mean *playing*. Not some untutored youngster struggling with the instrument or a rambling old has-been whose tongue and lips were failing, I thought. This was a true jazz virtuoso. But in public in Hyde Park? Astonishing. I quickly finished off my coffee and went in search of the unknown player.

I soon spotted a young man, in his late twenties I guessed, sitting on a low wall near the café. With shoulder-length hair and wispy beard above a cheese-cloth shirt, jeans and battered sandals, he had that rarely washed, slightly scruffy but pretty look that identified many of the hippies who were around at the time.

And playing a tenor sax that fitted him perfectly. Because this was no gleaming, fresh-out-of-the-case, instrument. It was dull and tarnished, with a few scratches and small dents, and not an inch of polished brass anywhere.

A younger woman sat next to him. Blonde and suntanned and wearing a mini-skirt, even though they were already out of fashion by then. But with legs like hers anything longer would have been a crime against feminine aesthetics. She seemed to have no other purpose than to hold his plastic box of reeds, roll his cigarettes and draw the attention of passers-by. Which she did very successfully without moving and further displaying her body. He would occasionally glance at her while he was playing and when he paused between tunes, I saw by his eyes that he was stoned.

A Dylan-style corduroy cap lay open at his feet. Almost half-filled with money. The usual coppers, but a lot of silver and even a few pound notes. And one splendid, lone fiver. Dropped there by someone with money and a true appreciation of jazz saxophone, I thought. A terrific return for his playing.

76

It was then I noticed he had picked the perfect spot for a solitary busker. The park was always full, especially at weekends, but the path leading from the boat-hire cabin and the café to Rotten Row and Knightsbridge was never less than busy. And on summer days like this, people were more than ready to stop, take a breather, eat their ice creams and listen for a while.

As I did. Standing entranced while he played another seven or eight songs. Starting with cool jazz from the 1940s and 50s and ending with swing and bebop. His range of genres and varied styles of playing was very impressive.

He eventually announced that he was taking a half hour drinks break. It was only then I realised that he was American. I approached him and introduced myself. Richard, I said. And I'm Ed, he replied. The young woman remained anonymous. Did he not know her name perhaps? Or in his stoned condition had he simply forgotten it?

I asked if he and his lady would like a cold drink. Yes, please, from both. She was English with a soft, middle-class accent. I went to the café and returned carrying three cold Cokes. When we had all taken our first, long drinks, I asked him if he was over here on holiday.

"No, man," he said with a lazy smile. "Came over on a mature student exchange and somehow never seemed to exchange back."

"So you're here illegally then Ed?" I asked, without thinking. Feeling foolish as soon as the words were out of my mouth.

He smiled again. "What's legal, man?" he said. "That all depends on your definition, yeah? Borders are just lines a bunch of old guys drew on their maps and those lines don't mean shit to me. I'm alive, free and a citizen of the world. What's more legal than that?"

I replied that in an ideal world I could only agree with him. But this was an imperfect world we lived in.

"Well, that's cool," he said. "Because I'm an imperfect human being. Kind've fits, no?

"I don't know what imperfections you do have," I said, "but playing the saxophone is definitely not one of them. Because I think you're phenomenal."

"Well, thanks man," he said with a little bow of acknowledgement. "And no offence you understand, but how would you know?"

"Because I'm a professional musician myself," I explained. "A session man. Keyboards, basic guitar and harmonica. I play with other professionals for a living and you're right in there with them. Better than a lot of them in fact. It's mostly rock and pop these days – that's where the money is - but jazz is my first and only real love. I heard Charlie Parker, Lester Young, Coltrane, and Sonny Rollins in what you were playing, *and* a better than average rendition of Coleman Hawkins' Body and Soul.

He nodded a couple of times and smiled. "But you missed Johnny Hodges."

"Not now you've mentioned him, I haven't" I said. "The sax part of 'Prelude To A Kiss' wasn't it? I missed it because the original was played on an alto sax, not tenor."

He nodded again, long and slow. "Yeah, you sure know your jazz, man."

"Tell me," I said, fascinated, "where did you learn to play like that?"

"My grandfather played sax in a local dance band. Weddings, bar mitzvahs, high school proms, you know, that kind've stuff. He started me when I was eight. Alto sax. Tenor was too big for me. In my teens I played in the school orchestra and local bands. The Alto is still my favourite but I can't afford two instruments. I got this one real cheap, so tenor it is for now."

"So, who do you play for now, Ed."

He waved his hand around the park. "The world, man," he said. "I play for the people, my fellow citizens."

I told him I could introduce him to lots of people in the business and in a few short months he could make enough to buy half a dozen saxophones.

He just smiled another dreamy smile. "Yeah, but I don't play for money, man. I just play for the love of the music. The love of the music is everything."

I raised my eyebrows, pointed to his cap and the money it contained.

He laughed. "There's a big difference though. You get paid by the man, the corporate suits, to produce music to make *them* profits. People are required to *buy* the music you create to make those profits. Here, I play for the people. For free. If they want to drop a couple of bucks in my cap to say they liked what they heard, then that's cool. They don't *have* to, you understand? Totally their own choice. I'm just a working man with my tool and a lot of working people give me a little money as a way of saying 'nice job'. Pure barter, man, human to human. Not *commerce*."

I told him I had intended to give him £20 but that I'd had a much better idea. I shook his hand and asked if he'd be in the same place next weekend.

He said that he would. "God willin' and the creek don't rise," he added with a smile. And picked up his sax again. The beautiful sounds followed me as I strolled off towards the Knightsbridge Underground station.

During the week I duly asked around my musician friends and was eventually introduced to a man who right then needed money a lot more than he needed his instrument. Sister heroin makes desperate sellers of all her users. I gave him £25 for a beautifully cared for Selmer alto sax, complete with solid case and cleaning kit.

I returned to the Serpentine the following weekend and sure enough, young Ed was in the same place, wearing the same clothes, with the same cap at his feet while he played the same glorious jazz. But with a different girl at his side. One who was equally tanned and beautiful as the other had been. Was the attraction him or the saxophone? Probably both, I decided.

During his break I approached him, exchanged greetings and handed him the case. He opened it and took the instrument out.

"Aw, man, an alto!" he said. Awe in his voice. Then paused. "But no way can I afford this."

I told him it was a gift and that it hadn't cost me much more than the twenty I was going to give him last weekend. I told him I considered a second-hand saxophone more than a fair return for the pleasure he'd given me.

He looked up at me and I swear there were tears in his eyes as he extended his hand. As I shook it he told me I was a *'dude amongst dudes'*.

"Now I can play Bird the way he should be played," he said, as he fitted the mouthpiece. He then played an ascending scale before launching into his version of Charlie Parker's "I Got Rhythm."

I sat and listened for while before leaving the park but returned with my son for the next three weekends in a row to listen and drop a fiver in his cap. And buy a cold Coke or two for him and his legion of young women. Where *did* he find them all, I wondered? But didn't dare ask.

Then that never-ending summer did finally end, the weather changed and though I returned five or six times, I never saw or heard him again. It left a surprising hole in my weekends, but I consoled myself with the thought that I had been privileged to hear him play so many times. Just for the love of the music. I still feel that.

THE LAST WALTZ

He was known as Waltzin' Davey by all the regulars at the dance hall and the pub next door. The doormen, the barmen, the cloakroom girls, and the girls who danced you a dance for a half a crown. And the local boys who didn't know him outside the hall and the girls they brought with them. They called him by the long version when he wasn't around but plain "Waltzer" to his face.

"Seen Waltzin' Davey tonight?" would turn in a second into *"Hey, Waltzer, how you doin?"* as he soft-shoe'd onto the dance floor.

And looked good as he did it, too. A shade under six feet, his slim frame moving quickly and lightly around the floor. Smarter even than the average, which was high in those days. His hair was always perfect, always in place, with a razor sharp parting. He always wore a dark blue or dark grey hand-made suit, just about fashionable, with three buttons, no vents and turn-ups on the trousers. A plain collar white shirt and narrow maroon tie held in place by a gold tie-pin finished everything off.

Everything, that is, apart from the spit-shined black shoes. Some of the older girls thought they were his father's patent leather dancing pumps, but they were just polished to a perfect high gloss finish. You could track his progress around the floor by those shoes.

But only on Tuesdays and Thursdays, and only for the Waltz. No Quicksteps, Tangoes or Foxtrots for Davey. Just the Waltz. Benny the Sax player asked him why, one night, and Davey just said that if there was such a thing as the rhythm of life, then the Waltz was it. Didn't know of any movement that compared to the one-two-three waltz sway and glide with a girl at your toes.

Benny looked for some sexual connotation there but couldn't find any in Davey's smiling face. And when he thought about it, found he couldn't disagree with him either. He looked at Davey in a different light after that.

But the best, and rarest thing was they all liked him. People darkened by the cynicism that grew in a dance hall and fuelled by the beer, Gin and Whisky from the pub next door. People who'd seen and heard everything their world could do and say. Much of it bad. They all liked him. The doormen because he was respectful and polite, talked quietly with them as equals, not menials with muscles. And never forgot their names.

The girls loved him. Even more polite with them than he was with the doormen, always attentive, always aware of them as individuals. Never made them feel the failure they felt when they looked inside themselves.

The best thing for the girls was that was he never held them too close as they danced. Never pulled them onto his thigh, never slid his hands low on their hips to squeeze their buttocks. And no pressing an unwanted erection against them like a lot of the other boys.

His particular favourite was Sylvia, the oldest of the girls. She said she was twenty eight but they all suspected she'd passed the dreaded thirty barrier. Her maternal attitude towards the girls reinforced her status as the leading lady. Always available for advice and help with contraception, and the odd unwanted pregnancy, a woman who seemed to know all the discreet clinics. *"No back-street butchers for my girls. Knitting needles is for wool and Gin's for drinking,"* was how she put it to them. And she always took in the odd stray girl who'd left home after a family row.

Short and small-boned, but with surprising breasts and an even more surprising tongue on her, she was proud of her figure, never missing an opportunity to tell the younger girls that she didn't need no girdle to hold her stomach in. She intimidated most of the young men who came.

But not Davey. He danced with her the first night anyone remembered seeing him. And they moved. Oh how they moved across that floor. Nothing touching except their clasped hands, her free one on his shoulder, his perfectly, lightly, in the small of her back guiding her gently with him.

And he danced at least five dances with her most nights after that. He bought her drinks in between and asked questions that showed a rare interest in her.

"Don't just talk about himself all the bleedin' time, like the others", she said. "Don't try to look down my dress, don't touch, he don't. He's lovely. And there's a bit of mystery about him as well. Says he's from Peckham but I don't believe him. Far too well-mannered for bleedin' Peckham."

"You bleedin' well fancy him, you do," Albert, the head doorman said one night. The only one in the place who could say something like that to her and not get a mouthful in return. They were of an age, Sylvia and Albert, six or seven years older than the rest of the crowd. And both of them had been married. Albert still was, although Sylvia's had ended long ago. Nobody seemed to know why.

"Drink, gambling and other women," she'd said one night, when someone dared ask her after the dance hall had closed. When they were all drunk on the champagne an Arsenal footballer had bought them. "It's ain't original," she said, "but then he never was that, not even in fucking bed."

Best of all, she could tie Albert's bow tie. Someone, his mother perhaps, had once told him that clip-ons were dead common and that real toffs only wore tie-ups. All the band wore clip-ons which somehow seemed to prove her point. And Sylvia knew how to do them perfectly. She'd fasten it, almost on tiptoes as her five feet one leaned into his six feet three.

"Look like a priest and a communicant," said Jimmy, who was a bad catholic boy. She'd fasten it, step back, pat the bow, pat his chest with the same hand, kiss the end of his nose and spin away to the floor.

Sylvia's relationship with Davey existed mostly in her imagination, driven partly by the comments of the other girls. But it was made real the night he defended her in the hall.

She was dancing with an older man, older than her and not one of the locals. A man who found the mix of drink and physical contact too much to handle. Davey and Will had first noticed him trying to kiss her neck and knead her breasts. Then she was struggling with him, dancing all but forgotten.

Davey was already moving as they danced towards him. And saw Sylvia suddenly push the man away. But the man was too quick for her. His right hand grabbed the neck of her dress as he stumbled backwards and ripped it apart, exposing her breasts and what passed for a bra, for all the world to see.

Davey covered yards before anyone else had moved. And reached them well before the man's fist could make contact with Sylvia's face. Davey kicked him, hard, behind one knee and the man folded, punch forgotten. Before he could drop, Davey spun on his left foot, up on his toes, swung his right leg in a wide arc and kicked the man full in the face, breaking his nose and sending him ten feet backwards against the front of the bandstand.

Benny dropped the sax from his mouth and signalled the band to stop playing. Davey dragged the man up by the hair and handed him to Albert.

"You're supposed to take *much* better care of her than that, you are," he said as Albert wrapped one arm around the man and started to carry him away. "It's what you're here for after all."

Nixon, the Jamaican drummer, played a little roll-riff and tapped a cymbal.

Albert stopped dead, dropped the man and looked round, staring at Davey. He moved towards him, pointing, and started to speak. But Davey just stood there, holding the stare and something about the look on his face stopped Albert cold.

Davey shook his head, took off his jacket and wrapped it around Sylvia's shoulders, buttoning it to cover her breasts. Then he bent and wiped the blood off his shoe with a paper serviette before he took her arm and walked her to the pub. Where he bought her large brandies and fed her cigarettes. And listened.

He took her home before the Hall closed and that was when they first realised he had a bit of money. Because he took her in a taxi. A quid at least to her place, God knows how much more then to his. To Sylvia's disappointment, he refused her offer to come up for a nightcap. But did it in a way that didn't cause her any offence.

"Said he didn't want to take advantage of me the state I was in," she told them the next night. "After what he did for me I'd 'ave done it with 'im in the bloody cab. Taken me knickers off there and then if he'd wanted… and whatever else he fancied as well. But he just held my hand and talked to me 'til we got there. Waited in the cab 'til I'd gone upstairs for a cardy and brought his jacket back. Then kissed me on the cheek before he went off home. Bit of class, he is. I tell you, he's not from bleedin' Peckham."

Which was what he'd told them all in the early days, when the curiosity was there. And that raised their eyebrows, because not many came from south of the river to the dance halls in those day. Not many people even went from Tottenham to Hammersmith, never mind across the Thames.

Confirmation that he had money came when Kenny spotted the label in his suit one night when Davey took his wallet out to pay for a round of drinks.

"Cecil fucking Gee," he said later, his voice a mixture of awe and envy. "Shaftesbury Avenue. I mean, who can afford hand-mades from Cecil Gee? Charge you three quid just to look in the bleedin' window that lot. Who *is* this bloke? And what *is* he?"

But that night changed relationships for good. Changed the balance between the pair of them and everybody else at the hall. He still only danced the Waltz, but now only ever with Sylvia. And took her home by taxi every time.

"Got to be givin' 'im one, 'ent she?" Jimmy said one night. "Well," he said when one or two shook their heads and smiled, "she's well up for it. Goes like a bunny, I've 'eard. Give 'er one meself, 'cos she's still pretty tasty for an old bird. Them tits is a bit special…"

He never heard Albert, never saw his fist, just felt something suddenly destroy his stomach. Something that laid him out vomiting on the floor and kept him away from the hall until Albert sent word it was safe to return.

"Never accepts my bloody invites when we get to my place, says he doesn't want to spoil it," she told Albert one night. "Says he enjoys it as it is and that if he sleeps with me, and he says he would, he fancies me well enough, but if he did it would change things completely. And he doesn't want that. The prick. The lovely bleedin' prick. Ah well, just have to live with it, I suppose," she snuffled as Albert wrapped a long, protective arm around her.

People accepted it as the norm all through that Summer. Until one Tuesday night, when he didn't appear. Sylvia didn't say a word to anyone, not even Albert, but she couldn't relax into the dancing. She was off hand with the customers, abusive with some, and when her language got too bad even for the band, the manager was called to pull her out for the night.

She went straight home, telling him where he could stuff her wages for the night. When he failed to appear again, on the Thursday night, she refused to dance at all, and walked out of the hall without a word to Albert or the others. The manager was for sacking her there and then, said he'd had it with her. He was used to the young ones coming over all emotional, they caused him enough grief without Sylvia starting.

But he shut up and went back to his office when Albert explained, publicly, what he would do to him if he ever thought that again, never mind said it. Albert found her in the pub next door and fed her Gin while he talked her round.

"Come on, Sylv," he said. "I mean, who'll fasten me bloody tie if you don't? he said. Can't be seen with me little dangly bits hangin' out all over the place, can I? I need you, girl."

That seemed to be the clincher because she came in to dance on the Friday. But wearing just a little bit more rouge, just a little bit more eyeliner and mascara. And a few more little, false smiles.

She joined them at the big table as they sat with brought-in drinks, waiting for the Hall to open. The conversation had barely started up again when the Manager walked over to them and slid the Daily Express onto the table. Open at page four.

Which contained a story about one Mrs Richard Hardy, of Croxted Road, Herne Hill, South London. Charged with murder for stabbing her husband to death with a kitchen knife after she'd caught him in their bed with another man. Caught him *inside* another man in their bed to be precise. The gender seemed to be much less significant than the fact of the marital bed, though.

According to the report, he was the Clerk in a Barristers' Chambers and she worked for a small finance house in the City. As usual on a Monday, she'd gone off to her night class. Accountancy: she was intent on improving her position at the company, she'd told the police. But the class had been cancelled at short notice because Mr Arthurs, the Accountant who took it, was ill. She'd refused the offer to join the others for a drink and had returned home for an unexpected night in with her husband.

Only to hear the equally unexpected but absolutely unmistakable sounds of the mattress, *her* mattress, complaining at the physical activity taking place. The fact that it happened in her bedroom, her bed, seemed to have far more significance for the lady than the deed she witnessed and the betrayal that was taking place.

There was a picture of her being led into a police station included in the article, together with another picture, taken on the Embankment by Temple Station, of the late Mr Richard Hardy. Or Waltzin' Davey as he was better known to his dance hall friends.

Time stopped. No-one said a word. No-one dared. They all turned to look at Sylvia and waited for the explosion. Which didn't happen. Instead, she sat, fists clenched as she read the article twice and studied the picture for long minutes afterwards. Then she stood up, kicked the chair back and looked at them all.

"At least *he* was fucking original", she said before she walked out of the hall and into the pub next door. Albert fingered his bow tie and slowly shook his head as he followed.

THE WEDDING DRESS

Most of my friends pitied me, laughed at me even, but I never found that the twice-weekly, after-school visits to my Grandmother's house were a chore.

'What do you want to spend time with an old woman like that for?' they asked me. *'What on earth do you find to talk about? She knows nothing.'*

Which she didn't, of course, not in the way they meant. She had absolutely no interest whatsoever in contemporary teen culture: the latest boy/girl singers, the fashion, the makeup, the boys. All the transient stuff that is so important to us teenage girls meant nothing to her. She made that clear and never referred to it, ever.

What they didn't understand – and I gave up trying to explain – was that she knew so much more. So much that I would never learn from my friends - or at school. She gave me a window into the past, *her* past and for some reason I never quite understood, I was fascinated by it all. And by her. So much so that what began as duty calls imposed on me by my parents, quickly became one of the highlights of my week.

Even though I was only sixteen and she was seventy-six, we related in ways I would never have thought possible, and I always came away with something new and different to think about. She was the only Socialist in our family, my parents being the palest form of Liberals who could see both sides of every social issue and built the fences to sit on so that they could see them more clearly.

But my Grandmother had strong opinions on everything. She was born of farming stock in the early twentieth century and left school when she was twelve to work on the farm where her family were tenants. And work she did. From four in the morning until nine at night, helping her mother with cooking, washing and cleaning as well as tending the vegetable gardens, milking the cows and looking after the other animals.

But she somehow knew from an early age that she was intelligent and bright. And suspected she was quite clever as well.

"I realised that ninety percent of what adults told me was complete drivel, my dear, made no sense to me at all. It was mainly designed to keep us children in our place. My parents, aunts and uncles and teachers were bad enough, but the priests were the worst. So I decided I had to read everything I could lay my hands on so that I could make my own mind up."

Which she did. She formed opinions that could only be changed by strong, cogent, intelligent argument. They were strongly held because they were based on a thorough examination and analysis of all the information that was available to her. I didn't agree with everything she said, of course, but I don't remember her ever having a second-hand opinion on anything. She would happily disagree with politicians, newspaper leader writers, teachers, the doctor and, most especially, the local priest, a man she seemed to regard with a particular haughty disdain.

She also enjoyed annoying my father, her son, by constantly chiding him about his inability to form a strong opinion or make a decision and by dismissing his wife as a *'soggy doormat'*. He, in turn, was infuriated by her frequent definitive pronouncements on issues that he found impossibly complex.

Even more so when she mocked him for being a psychiatrist. Which she often did. "A dealer in male, penis-centred, masturbation-originated, mumbo-jumbo, neither use to man nor beast," was one of her milder declarations. When he complained that she fit the analysis due to the issues she had caused him as a child and was continuing to struggle with as an adult, she was totally dismissive. *'You really are old enough to take ownership of your own problems and deal with them. There comes a point, surely, when you simply cannot keep on blaming someone else. Or does Freud have nothing to say about that?'*

After one occasion when I'd heard him mutter something about pitying her husband, I asked her about my Grandfather, who'd died when I was four.

"Your Grandfather, dear? Well, he was a nice man. He was a good man, actually, but ultimately a weak man. And he loved me without being able to describe what love is. And he left all the decisions to me."

I laughed. "But I thought that would've suited you down to the ground, Vera."

"Yes, it did. Of course it did. But in the rural life then, my dear, it was always the women who made the decisions, who managed absolutely everything. The men worked, tended to the field work, ensured the money kept coming in, yes, but that was the easy part. Women had everything else to do for the home, the children, the animals, managing the money - and the men themselves, of course, though they'd never admit it. We always were, and still are, the stronger sex, whatever they might try to tell you. You need to remember that as you move through life."

Which I did. And I also never forgot another lesson she taught me.

"Never judge a person by what they are, the position they hold in society. Judge them by *who* they are, their values, behaviour and how they treat other people. Do they give *love?* That's the real test you know."

And that proved invaluable to me.

She was a tiny, bird-like woman who always seemed to be busy in the house, or in the garden when the weather was good. I never saw her relaxing except for the hour or so before she went to bed when she would sit in 'her' armchair with a book and a glass of Port. Sometimes accompanied by a digestive biscuit, but most often with a bar of chocolate.

When I mentioned to her the latest warnings about alcohol and sugar, she was at her most dismissive.

"Men dear. They're trying to turn our health into a commodity. To make money from it. And to make us feel guilty. They should always use the words '*to excess*' when talking about any foodstuffs but they don't of course. Because that would have the effect of allowing people, like me, to continue with their regular habits. I've been drinking Port and eating chocolate in reasonable doses all my life, and if that's what's going to kill me dear, well, there are many worse things to die from. I refuse to be a commodity and I refuse to allow them to turn my little pleasures into guilty habits. *Men!*"

So, her body might have been old, but her mind wasn't. Apart, that is, from her apparent inability to remember my name. Most of the time she called me "my dear" or just "dear". But she insisted that I call her Vera and not gran or grannie. When I asked why, she simply said that she was a woman with a name, not a specimen with a label.

"But you never use my name, ever, Vera. That doesn't seem fair somehow."

She just laughed. "Privilege of age my dear, one of the few we have."

My father, though, was addressed by his full name every time. He was Fred or Freddie to his friends, but she always called him Frederick. He complained once that the use of his full name was a form of bullying, a reminder of the former power balance in the relationship.

"*Former*, Frederick?" she'd replied. "*Former?* More psychiatrist's nonsense? There's nothing remotely *former* about it. I'm your mother and you're my son. And so it always shall be. You may be a grown man, now… or so you keep telling me. But you are still my son. The power balance in our relationship remains the same, always will do, and bullying simply doesn't come into it."

Her treatment of my father reflected her views on the difference between the sexes, views that would have left many published Feminists struggling in her wake. She believed in emancipation (as she still quaintly called it) but also had strong views about the correct way for women to behave in many of life's circumstances.

Central to that was her attitude towards sex, something that was graphically reinforced when I called round one particular day after school. As I walked through the front gate I saw smoke rising up from behind the house.

I dropped my bag and ran round to the back garden only to find that Vera had a large fire going. And was standing over it poking it with a stick.

I grabbed her arm. "Vera, what are you doing? You frightened the life out of me. Thought the house was on fire."

"Nonsense, dear. It's just a garden fire."

"But what's that in it? Doesn't look like any old garden rubbish to me."

"It's my wedding dress, dear."

I stood, mouth open in astonishment. "What? Your wedding dress? But why? It's an antique. Silk, lace, pearls and everything," I eventually managed to say. "And you always said I could wear it at my wedding."

"Silly girl, I've removed the pearls. And it's not appropriate for you now, dear."

"*What?* Not appropriate? What on earth do you mean? And what's *appropriate* mean anyway? It doesn't mean anything these days."

She sighed, then turned and walked away. She sat down on the garden seat and gestured for me to sit beside her.

"You know Mrs Harris who runs the Post Office, her daughter got married last week?"

I nodded, wondering where this was going.

"I was talking to her last month and she said her daughter had no money for a dress, neither did she, so I said I would loan her mine. And I did and she wore it to the Church. But I've since discovered that she was pregnant when she got married so she'd no right to wear white at all. But she did. Her mother brought it back today, but it's spoiled now. I just can't bear to have it in the house again."

I was astonished for the second time in minutes. This didn't fit with her views at all. Because she'd talked to me about contraception, masturbation, even dildos. When I looked surprised at that, she just snorted and said, "What, you think we old folk didn't have sex? How on earth do you young people think you all *got* here for goodness sake? And we didn't only have sex within marriage either. Or exclusively with males."

The thought of my Nan involved in lesbian sex? I was beyond shocked, and I swear my jaw dropped. Whether it did or not, she laughed when she saw the expression on my face.

"Just because a number of your friends find it so much easier to come out today does *not* mean that your generation invented lesbians, my dear. The true sisterhood *did* exist back in my day."

"Yes, I know, but…

"Do you imagine, for example, that some of the Suffragettes weren't lesbians?"

"I hadn't honestly thought about it before, Vera, but now you mention it… Sorry, it's just I'm so shocked Vera."

"Well, that's an awful lot more to do with your sensibilities than my behaviour, dear."

"Maybe, but the thought of you, the mental image of you doing *that*."

Vera snorted. "Oh piffle," she said. "You have no idea how difficult it was to be anything other than a compliant, dutiful wife when I was your age. Very few doors were open to women, but they were all fully closed to lesbians. If I was your age now, I think I would probably be lesbian…" She paused for a few seconds. "No, I'm sure I would because when I did *indulge,* my close friends criticised me and poked fun at me, but they just didn't know what they were missing."

I shook my head and smiled. "You know what, Vera, I'll never look at you the same way again. Never."

"Good. At least you've learned something today young lady."

"Not to judge anybody until you know their full story, you mean?"

"Exactly! Now what were we talking about before you took me on that lovely diversion?"

I had to think for a moment while I cleared weird visions of Vera from my head.

"Oh, I know," I said, "we were talking about not wearing a white wedding dress if you've had sex before marriage. I don't understand why it matters any more, Vera. Lots of women have sex before marriage these days and quite a few are carrying when they go up the aisle. Thought you had a more broad-minded view about sex anyway."

She smacked me lightly on the leg.

"You need to listen more closely, dear. What I was referring to were society's - and by that I mean *men's* - attitudes towards sex. Repressed, male-dominated attitudes that need to change so that we can discuss everything about sex more openly and in a more intelligent way. That contraception should be freely available for women so that they can make their own choices. That abortion should be the woman's decision and hers alone. It's her body after all. *That* was the sort of thing I was talking about. What I did *not* say was that sex should be given out like sweets to anyone who comes along with their hand out - or their appendage, to be more precise."

She pointed at me repeatedly as if to emphasise the points she was making.

"Because it's not so much about sex, then, dear, it's about love and respect. Respect for traditions, yes, but more for yourself. Because sex doesn't necessarily have anything to do with love. The whole free-sex thing? Feminism has got that wrong in my view. You shouldn't give your body, and part of yourself along with it, to just anybody, whenever you or they feel like it, get the urge so to speak. Do that as a young woman and you'll get no respect. And that eventually means that you won't respect yourself."

I started to speak but she stopped pointing and raised her hand to stop me.

"Most men, especially young men, only want one thing from a girl… no, no, don't look at me like that. It's an old cliché I know, but I believe it's none the less true for that. It's teenage hormones driving them, not their brains. They want that one thing and when they've got it they just move on to the next girl – or the needy ones don't. They just cling on and drain all the teenage fun out of you. And you? You're left a little less complete than you were. But you should know my views, we've discussed this same subject many times before."

"But your dress was going to be mine, you said so," I objected.

"Well… you've had sex already, dear, so you couldn't have used it either – or if you had then I wouldn't have come."

"But how…"

"…did I know? My dear, I see you every week and I know all the signs. I know when a young woman has, *blossomed,* as the old ones used to say. You've certainly done that these past few months. You are positively *blooming.* It was the young Williams boy, wasn't it?"

"Jesus, Vera…"

It was, of course, the young Williams boy. Richard. He and I had been enjoying ourselves in sexual discovery for more than three months by then.

"But since it's burned now, dear, this conversation is all rather pointless don't you think?"

With that she walked over to the fire, gave it one more vigorous poke and walked off into the house.

I did eventually fall in love. And got married. Not to Richard. But I wore my own (non-white) dress.

And Vera came.

SISTER LOVE

The young nurse walked out of the ward, still wearing her uniform, bag over her shoulder and approached the reception desk. The older nurse on duty looked up and smiled.

"Hey, Jen. You finally getting away then? What was the problem this time?"

The young nurse scowled. "*Mister* Campbell. Again. Insisted I stay until he finished his round. Again. And you know how he talks."

"I do. And no point telling him you've already been on fourteen hours."

"He wouldn't even hear me," Jen said. "Doesn't even *see* us nurses unless he's cocked something up and needs us to put it right for him."

The older nurse laughed. "Yeah, you're right about that. But never mind, you're off now. Going anywhere nice?"

"Bed would be the nicest," Jen said, "but fat chance of that for a while. Got to call in on me nan."

"Oh, right. Best of luck with that. Need your bed even more after." She paused. "You're not changing out of your uniform?"

"Nah, can't be arsed," Jen said.

"You know this hospital rules are no uniforms outside the grounds."

"Yeah, I know, but what are they gonna do, sack me? There aren't enough of us as it is for them to do that. I'll change at me nan's – or not bother 'til I'm home. Night."

"Night love. You take care. See you in the morning."

Jen took the lift down, walked out and crossed the car park into the street. Where, thank heavens, a bus was due in three minutes. She nodded at some of the other nurses waiting.

"Hi Jen," one of them said, "you late off as well? What happened?"

"Mr bleedin' Campbell happened, that's what," she said. "Had to stay on til' he'd finished his round."

"Him again," another nurse said. "My heart sinks whenever I see he's on my ward. Never stops bloody talking. You'd think he didn't have a home to go to."

"He hasn't, really," Jen said. "His wife died two years ago."

"Died of boredom I shouldn't wonder, listening to him rabbit on non-stop."

"Bit harsh, Chloe."

"Yeah maybe but tell me I'm wrong."

Thankfully the bus pulled up, sparing her any more of that. She climbed on, flashed her card and sank into a seat. Put the bag on her lap and settled back.

No! Musn't close my eyes, she thought. Miss me stop and be even later getting to nan's. Be bad enough as it is without being even later. She sat up straight and looked out of the window at shops and people in a desperate effort to stay awake.

Which she managed to do. Got up at her nan's stop, said thank you to the driver and climbed off. She walked a few hundred yards up the main road then turned left and approached her nan's block of flats. Took a deep breath and pressed the bell. Old cow *still* won't give me a key she thought. And could hear her saying it. *"Don't want nobody able to walk into me place without me knowing. Wouldn't feel safe."*

101

When the buzzer sounded, the old woman turned away from the TV, rolled her wheelchair across the room to the internal phone and picked up the receiver.

"Who's that?" she shouted.

"Only me, nan."

"Who?"

Oh, here we go again, the girl thought. Yet another shouting match just so she could have a conversation with the old woman. She wears me out, she does.

"Me, nan. It's Jen," she shouted back. "Me. Your granddaughter. You remember?"

"'Course I remember me own granddaughter! I ain't gone senile, have I? But you're late! Supposed to be here two hours ago you were."

Lord help us and save us.

"Well I'll be even later if you don't buzz me in, won't I?"

The old woman pressed the buzzer then wheeled herself back to face the TV. A few moments later the young woman walked in wearing her blue nurse's uniform. She was a very pretty woman in her early twenties but with stress and tiredness showing in her face, and especially her eyes.

Fifteen-hour shifts do nothing for a good-looking young woman. She wore no makeup and no jewellery apart from tiny silver ear studs. She kept her hair short, in a very stylish boy's cut.

The old woman stared at her.

"You've had your hair cut!" she shouted. "All that lovely hair. Halfway down your back it was. Look like a bleedin' boy you do now. What you wanna go and do something like that for, eh?"

102

"Because it was such a pain having to tie it up before every shift, nan, that's why. And it only takes me five minutes to wash and dry 'stead of an hour. Got sick of all the hassle. So I had it all off."

Which was the truth of it. And, surprisingly, she found she loved it. Loved the look and the fact that it was so much easier to manage. One of the patients, an old man, said she just reminded him of somebody called Twiggy. But she had no idea who that was. Until she Googled it, of course, and discovered what a compliment she'd been paid.

"Look nan," she said. She shook her head vigorously from side to side and when she stopped, her hair was still perfectly back in place. "That's how easy it is now."

Her nan just narrowed her eyes and growled. The young woman laughed and kissed her on the forehead before reaching over and turning the TV down.

"Oi! Can't hear it now, can I?"

"That's the point, nan. Way you've got that thing blasting out, can't hear meself think never mind hear you."

"Well I'm deaf, aren't I?"

"Really? Never have guessed. Surprised the neighbours aren't deaf as well by now. Just hope they like the same programmes you do, that's all. And where's your hearing aids, anyway. You're supposed to wear them all the time."

"What, them things? Hate 'em, I do. And they look stupid. I ain't being seen with them pink things sticking out me ears. People'd just laugh."

"But you never go out anywhere, nan, nobody'll ever see them, so what's it matter?"

103

"Matters to me," the old woman said. "Never mind all that, where you bin anyway, girl? Said you'd be here hours ago!"

"Duh!' the young woman said, spreading her arms and presenting her uniform. "Where's it *look* like I been, eh?"

"Rubbish! Told you before, you should leave when your shift's finished. You're entitled. My Ted always did."

"But he worked in the docks, nan, not a hospital. Bit of a difference. Didn't have responsibility the way I do. And the dockers? That lot, most of the time nobody knew if they was at work or not."

"Yeah came and went as they pleased they did. No bosses tellin' them what to bleedin' do. Kings they were, the London dockers."

"They weren't kings all those days they had to stand around hoping to get picked to work, were they? You didn't get picked, you didn't earn any money. No wonder they was all at it. Anyway, there's no more kings now though is there, nan? Got rid of the lot once all them containers came in."

"Retainers? What you on about? They weren't on no retainers. Had to work for everything they got. Like you said, the old days, turn up in the morning see if you got picked for the day. You didn't? No work and no money come in. Not like you young 'uns today. Got it easy you lot."

"Not retainers nan," she said. "Con… oh never mind. But it's different for me, I can't just walk out, can I?"

"Don't see why not," the old lady shouted. "Disgusting I calls it. Work you all hours just to suit them. And don't pay you for the extras neither. Good job you ain't married with kids. Blokes wouldn't put up with that."

The younger woman sighed. They'd had this conversation so many times before. And each time as pointless as the one before. It wasn't just the old woman's deafness; it was as if her brain just couldn't remember previous conversations. Early onset? She did wonder at times. More than her life was worth to even hint at it of course.

"Not to suit *them*," she said, "the managers, I mean, it's the doctors. If they need you, you have to stay. And the patients, nan. Can't just leave them in the middle of something. Told you before, it doesn't work like that. How'd you like it if it was you in there and the nurse walked off in the middle of dispensing drugs, giving you a bed bath or something?"

The old lady grunted.

"Anyway, she been round yet?"

"That sister of yours you mean? Yeah, came this afternoon, just after dinner."

"She okay?"

"Huh, that one? Seen her look better. When she was five probably. Thin, scruffy as usual. And sort of shivery she was. Sniffin' all the time. Still taking that bleedin' stuff I reckon. Be the death of her that will."

"Yes, nan. But she said she'd leave something here for me. Did she?"

"Yeah. Said she'd left it in back there."

"She say anything to you about it? 'Cos she wouldn't tell me what it was."

"Not really," the old woman said. "You know what that one's like. Just said, *'this is it, Jen'll be round for it later'*. Went through the back."

"But *where* in the back, nan?"

105

"In the spare bedroom I think."

"She didn't say nothin' else?"

"What? What've I just bleedin' told you? That's all she said. In between sniffin' and wipin' her bleedin' nose o'course. Borrowed a tenner off me, nicked twenty of me fags then left. There was a car."

"A car? What?"

"You deaf?" the old woman shouted. "Thought that was supposed to be me. A *car*, I said and a car I meant. Outside. Waitin' for her. Drove off when she went out."

"Whose was it?"

"I dunno, do I? How would I? Ain't seen 'im before. Shifty looking bloke, though. Head shaved like they do these days. But white, he was. Thought he was a black, her fella."

"Can't keep track, these days nan. You know what she's like. Last one I met was black though. Jamaican. Nice guy. From Greenwich, he was."

"*Greenwich*? Didn't think they had no blacks over there."

"Jesus nan, we're in the twenty first century now. They're not stuck in ghettos in Notting Hill and Brixton anymore."

The old lady growled. "I know it's the twenty first bleedin' century. Don't have to like it though, do I? And agree with everythin' that goes with it. 'Cos they shoulda kept them there. We knew where they was then. Knew where *we* was, come to that. Not surprised he was a blackie, though. How she gets all that stuff she bleedin' takes."

"*Nan!* He's not a bloody drug dealer, okay? He's a lovely fella, he is. He's a carpenter, got his own little business. And he's bought a place for him and his sister. Doin' alright, he is. Be a cryin' shame if she's split from him. And besides, white guys have been known to deal drugs you know. 'Specially round here."

The old lady wheeled around to face the TV again. "You know what I mean."

The young woman sighed. Yes, I do know what you mean, she thought. This family of mine's all the same. No wonder mum and dad are so screwed up having been raised by this woman. And how me and Sis had loads of Black and Asian friends all the way through school I'll never know.

"So, you been through to have a look, nan? And don't you *dare* turn that telly up again!" she shouted as the old woman reached for the remote.

"*Me?* No. What do I wanna have a look at whatever it is for, eh? Nothin' to do with me, is it? Told me she was leavin' somethin' for you, said you be round for it later, so why'm I goin' to poke me nose in, eh?"

"No 'course not, nan. Silly me."

"What you say?"

"Nothing, nan. Did dad know she was here?"

"Your Dad? *Him?* Why would he bleedin' know? Why would I tell him? *How* would I tell him? Ain't seen him in months. God knows where that one is these days. Wouldn't be interested anyway, would he? Not in anything she's doing. Not anymore."

"Mum?" she asked, trying to keep the irritation out of her voice. "Does she know?"

"Your Mum? Well yeah, course I told your Mum. Why wouldn't I?" She shook her head at what she clearly thought was a stupid question.

"No reason. So has *she* been round?"

"Not yet. Come round later she said. Too busy today. Huh! I know her busy. Didn't tell me his name though."

"Eh? His name? Didn't have to be a bloke, nan. Could've been anything."

"Know me own daughter don't I?" Not as if she's workin', is she?"

"So when? Did she say?"

"Not properly. Later on's all she said. About nine I think. Which means after eleven, knowing her. You hangin' round for her then?"

"I dunno. Maybe… depends on what you've got to eat, really. So it's still here then?"

"Course it is, stupid. If I haven't even been to look, where else would it bleedin' be, eh?"

"You know, sometimes you really do my head in, nan!"

"Don't be so bleedin' touchy! You asked and I told you. Just like your mum, you are," she grumbled.

The young woman shook her head. "I'll just go through and get it, then, will I?" she said as she walked through to the bedroom.

"That it?" the old woman asked when she came back with a small bundle in her arms, wrapped in a pillowcase.

"Well yeah, pretty sure it is. Somehow don't think this could be yours."

"Why? What is it?"

"It's a baby, nan, what's it look like?"

"A baby? Bugger me. All this time, and I never heard no bleedin' baby."

"You wouldn't, nan. It's dead."

"I know I'm deaf, don't I? Still think I'd have heard a baby crying."

"Not *deaf*, Nan. I said it was *dead*!"

"*Dead?* What's she doin' bringin' her dead little bastard round here for, eh? And what she expect you to do with it?"

She shook her head and thumped her fists on the arms of her wheelchair.

"You'll have to take it with you," she said. I ain't havin' no coppers and the bleedin' social round here. You can get rid, can't you?"

"I don't know, do I nan? Because I hadn't a clue what it was. She just said she was dropping off something here for me. Asked me to pick it up. I haven't spoken to her for about a year so I didn't even know she was pregnant. That's if it's hers, of course."

"Talk silly. 'Course it's hers. Who else's it gonna be?"

"I've no idea nan. But we don't know for sure it's hers. And anyway, doesn't have to be a little bastard. She might've gotten married."

The old woman snorted. "Who'd marry that one, I ask you. So, are you gonna tell me? What is it?"

"Eh? What do you mean?"

"The baby o'course. What else, stupid? What is it, boy or girl? You do know how to tell the bleedin' difference, don't you? You bein' a nurse an' all."

"Oh! yeah, sorry. Hang on a sec." She pulled open part of the cloth it was wrapped in.

109

"It's a little boy, nan."

"What colour is it?"

"What *colour*? Jesus, nan. Well… it's brown. Yeah, sort of a pale brown. Milky coffee like."

"Well there you go, then. Told you. Explains everything."

She wheeled away and turned the volume on the TV back to maximum.

The young woman sighed, shook her head and sat down on the sofa. Still cuddling the dead baby.

THE DEATH OF LOVE

Two old men sat quietly on the balcony of a Barcelona apartment looking out over the sea. Two glasses of white wine sat on the table between them. The bottle resting in a bucket of ice. A bottle of Brandy was also in evidence. In front of them on the table were two packets of Ducados and two identical Zippo lighters. Both men were chain-smoking. The sun was going down as they watched people leaving the beach.

Neither man had spoken for half an hour or more. But it was a comfortable silence. The silence of lifelong friends who had said everything important there was to say, and neither had any interest in talking simply for the sake of it. As is the case with old friends they had many *"do you remember when?"* conversations but they were usually about strokes they'd pulled. Memories that brought smiles and laughter. These two men didn't do regrets. Regrets were for losers.

One man, Jamesy, finished his wine, stubbed out his cigarette, and stood up.

"That's it for me, my old son, I'm off to bed. Don't stay up too long, will you?"

The other man nodded and reached for the Brandy as Jamesy stepped through the sliding doors into the apartment.

* * * * *

They were Jackson and James. Jackson, called Jake, because even at school he had hated the name his snobbish mother had given him. Dreamed he would live up to a good name, Mum did. Never thought about the potential beatings he would get at school because of it. But only potential. Because he had an intensity, a ferocity, that frightened off all but the oldest and hardest amongst them. And he handled himself so well against those few, held his ground and never took a backward step, that they respected him for it and often befriended him afterwards. Even after handing out a beating. Such were the ways of the playground and the street.

James was called just that, or more often, Jamesy. But never Jim or Jimmy. Not because he was fearless in the same way as Jake, but because he was considerably more lethal. And kids smelt that. They knew him. Recognised him. The one who would bide his time. Wait for the moment when he could exact his revenge. Never face to face. Always prepared it, planned it, so that he had the advantage.

There was a coldness about him, a vicious objectivity, that perfectly complemented Jake's wilder tendencies. Even the best of the teachers, while acknowledging their obvious intelligence, called them animals and predicted they would both come to *very* bad ends.

But the oddest thing about it all wasn't their different natures, it was that they had completely different home backgrounds. And the reverse of what everyone expected. Jake, the real animal, his dad was an Estate Agent, had his own business. And a huge, detached, five-bedroom house. With only a younger brother and sister to fill it. Private space, personal possessions, independence, Jake had all of that. And took it for granted. He knew other kids didn't have the same, but he didn't think about it, didn't judge them by it.

Jamesy's dad, on the other hand, was a dock worker and they lived in a three-bedroom flat in a Council block in Bermondsey. Two bedrooms for six kids. And the grandad. Jamesy didn't know what privacy was. Personal space wasn't a concept he understood. It simply didn't exist for him at home. That was a large part of the reason he spent so much time on the street. He only came home when he wanted to since nobody seemed to notice, or care, whether he was there or not.

Five kids had a bath together, watched over by Jamesy — when he was there. That was normal. Boys and girls together. He knew the difference between the two sexes by the time he was three. One had a bit that dangled, the other didn't. Simple. And that never bothered him. The only thing that did was whether the youngest would drown in the nightly water-based mayhem. Jamesy looked after her. He was the carer. The protector. Though he would have punched you silly if you'd ever said that to him.

As for possessions, he didn't begin to understand that some weren't for sharing. '*Mine*' and '*yours*' were alien concepts to the young boy who quickly learned that if you had something special you wanted to keep from the rest of the tribe, then you had to find, or create, hiding places. Inside the flat was best, but difficult.

Then he saw a movie and a cut floorboard gave him what he needed. Outdoors was easier because there were still a few bits of war damaged property around, filled with natural hiding places. Not too safe from other sharp kids though. He quickly learned that. So underneath the floorboards became his private space.

Physical retribution from the father was normal. Flat of the hand, fist or leather belt, depending on the mood he was in, or the seriousness of the offence committed. And, like many kids he knew, you made yourself scarce when he came home from the pub with a skinful. Which was a regular occurrence and their mum bore the brunt of it.

But as a kid, you made your choices, he learned early. Do something you wanted badly enough and take the beating or decide it wasn't worth it. Big decisions, adult decisions for a boy his age.

Yet those two boys, the complex and opposite mix that they were, individually and collectively, became instant friends at Primary School. Started talking the first day in the playground and were never separated. Jake was 'adopted' street whereas Jamesy was born and raised on it. He just naturally knew and understood the way of the world they inhabited without having to think about it at all. It was in-bred.

114

Jake, on the other hand, had to learn it all. But he had a good teacher in Jamesy and he was a quick learner. So they complemented each other perfectly although they never really understood that. Never even thought about the fact that they were both natural rebels. Their brows would have furrowed if anyone had said that to them, but that's exactly what they were.

And natural, fearless, adventurers. There was an old Vicarage in the area. Huge gardens. High brick walls. Of all the kids, they were the ones who dared climb the walls and steal apples and pears from the orchard. Jake, being Jake, would have taken the spares, the ones they couldn't eat themselves, and just given them away to their mates. But not Jamesy. No way he would have that.

"If they haven't the balls to get in there and nick 'em for themselves, they can bleedin' well pay for them" he said.

And pay for them they did. And quite happily it seemed. A couple of pence per apple and pear but it all mounted up. Kept them in fags at threepence for a single fag and a match from a local newsagent who would sell to a five-year-old if the kid had the money. With some cash left over. An early lesson for Jake. One that he never forgot. Because it was the beginning of their criminal career.

But the money for the cigarettes wasn't always needed. Jamesy used to steal them whenever he was anywhere near an open packet and the owner wasn't. Or when his Grandad, who was slowly going gaga, was there but not aware. Sometimes he'd take the whole packet safe in the knowledge that when the old man complained about his missing fags, his mum and other family members would shake their heads and tell him he must have smoked them all. Even the protests made in his lucid moments were always ignored. And learning this, Jake realised that almost anything was possible given nerve and the right circumstances. He never forgot that, either.

The best, though, was when Jamesy walked into the pubs and clubs collecting bets for his uncle, who was a street bookie. The men were so concerned about their bets, often arguing amongst themselves about their choices, their successes and failures, they never once noticed his hands lifting packets from the jackets that hung loose on the chairs. Or the ones that lay on the seats beside them. And if they were playing cards, which they often were, he would lift some cash from the piles on the table as well.

Subsequent accusations about who'd nicked whose bloody fags, or nicked whose cash, never centred on Jamesy. Why would they? He was only eleven years old after all, practically invisible. And they were all friends of his uncle and father.

Jake didn't need to take those risks. Life was simpler for him. If he couldn't steal money from his mum's purse - and it was a rare day that he couldn't - he'd just beat up any kid who had fags, money, or anything else he fancied, really.

Those who didn't have big brothers just had to swallow it. Those who did often called them in. But Jake had spent, smoked or sold whatever he'd taken so a fight was inevitable. Those he won, fine. Those he didn't, well, he never complained, never cried, just took his punishment and got on with life.

"Long as I'm in front, what's the problem taking a few lumps?" was the way he explained it to Jamesy.

They hardly spent any of the money. Didn't need to at their age. Apart from the few fags they had to pay for, comics and sweets were the staple needs at eleven and twelve. And a lot of the time they also took from other kids or nicked from shops. But not in their own part of London. They were already too well known in their manor to get away with that.

So the money they made simply accumulated. At Jake's house. No need for hiding places there, he told Jamesy. Neither parent ever went into his room if he wasn't there. Something Jamesy also found totally alien.

He trusted Jake with it. Trusted him absolutely. But Jake said that wasn't right. He'd taken one of the ledgers from his dad's office and noted down everything they made. It's the way it's done, he said when Jamesy protested it wasn't necessary. Proper record. So we both know what's what. He showed Jamesy the ledger every Sunday night. Red line drawn, another week's takings to be entered.

But a couple of years on, a box in Jake's bedroom wasn't doing it. Too much money. Because they'd started thieving properly instead of just shop lifting. They collected scrap for a while but gave it up as a bad job when the scrappy only gave them pennies. Because they were kids. But as the teen years progressed so did their thieving.

Just like most kids who entered the life, they had started by 'hoisting', working as a typical pair of spontaneous chancers snatching a bird in the bush, whatever the bird was or whatever bush it happened to be sitting in.

With clothing as one of the shoplifters' best items. They were good at it because hoisting is graft, a nerve-racking experience. And nerve was something they had in spades. They were forever on their toes, missing no opportunity and nothing of value being left unnoticed or untouched.

And then they graduated to breaking and entering, or 'creepin' as it was known back then. But only business premises. Never private houses. Because they all had neighbours behind nearby windows. And you never knew who might be sleeping upstairs while you were creeping around, or when people might come home.

And anyway, it was easy enough to get into shops in those days. Ridiculously so. Few security grilles and no CCTV. Some places didn't even have Chubbs. Just basic locks. Locks that a smart boy like Jamesy learned to pick very easily.

They took small stuff mainly. Anything they could carry because they didn't have a car or van to move it in. Clothes, shoes, cigarettes, alcohol, whatever was to hand. Transported it in a handcart at first. Nicked from the city market. Too easy. Two kids pushing an old cart? What could be more natural?

Then Jamesy remembered the pubs. He was invisible again. You can do anything if you're invisible he told Jake. And they're easy to get into. They duly cleaned out a till or two where the owner had been too lazy, forgetful, or pissed, to empty it overnight.

They ended up with over five hundred pounds. Enough to buy a house in those days. More than enough to open a bank account, Jake told him. Mum'll open it for me at the bank she uses, he'd said when Jamesy snorted at the thought of them two walking in anywhere and asking to open an account. Mum'll never look at it he said, she promised me that, and then as soon as we're old enough we'll get a joint account.

That early money also funded their social life. First came the dance halls. Mainly the Locarno, staying safe up West - although there were a few battles even so. But they never went to the Royal in Tottenham or the Hammersmith Palais. Way too far from home for a Bermondsey boy like Jamesy who thought Hammersmith was in a different country.

The halls were followed by the clubs in Soho. Always dressed as sharp as, in their handmade mohair suits, collar and tie and good shoes. And with expensive haircuts – no local barber for these two. Pulled their fair share of birds, as well as making some early alliances with several likeminded chaps who also reckoned having steady, honest jobs, working for poor wages was no way to live your life. Alliances that would serve them well in the future.

119

After a couple of years Jamesy reckoned they'd used up all their luck in their criminal dealings. To avoid becoming too well known and nicked as a result, he said, they had to find a new area of thievery and new fences. Jake wasn't so sure. He was having fun as well as making money.

Fun? That didn't enter into it where Jamesy was concerned. To him it was business, and serious business at that. So he carefully explained that the chances of being grassed were becoming too great because they were using the same old fences to shift the stuff.

As ever, Jake listened to his friend. Which is when they moved up to nicking cars. Quick and easy that was as well back in the day. No fool proof locks and alarms back then. And plenty of them left unlocked as well. Especially in the better parts of London where high value motors were the norm. And those areas became their regular hunting grounds.

Jaguars were their favourite pick because a nice Mk II Jag was the chosen getaway vehicle for many serious villains. And motors were easy to dispose of. Passed on to the many back-street dealers under the railway arches. No advertising them for sale - surest way to get nicked that was - and no questions asked by the seasoned men who took their spoils.

Nick them at ten at night, deliver before eleven and the theft wouldn't be discovered until nine or ten the next morning. If that. By which time, the car was a different colour, had new plates and sometimes was in a different county. And the boys pocketed large fistfuls of greasy tenners and twenties each time.

Unlike the scrappies, the old guys under the arches didn't care that they were kids; all they were interested in was the quality of the metal. And they quickly realised these two kids knew quality when they saw it. So much so that for a while they were nicking them to order for the two guys who ran the biggest of the archway businesses.

Then, just when they'd celebrated their twentieth birthdays, they hit the jackpot. The mother lode. With one big, totally unplanned score. In a side street just off a main square in the heart of London, where they'd taken to wandering around, investigating the wider world north of the river. Learning how the rich lived. Rolled a few drunks and dipped a few pockets and bags, but that was all. Serious breaking and entering hadn't entered their minds.

Until that one night, Jamesy picking a lock on a Jewellers for a laugh. Both ready to scarper when the alarm went off.

Nothing.

They looked at each other in silent question. Twenty seconds later, Jamesy realised the door wasn't even locked. Used his elbow to push down on the handle because even as teenagers they knew all about fingerprints. Still no alarm. Words weren't exchanged. A look and a nod were enough. They slid inside and Jamesy noticed that the key was there in the lock. Huh? He quickly locked the door behind them.

He went through the back and unlocked the door that led into an alley.

"*In case there's some kinda silent alarm and any coppers came to the front,*" Jamesy said. "*We slip out the back, into the alley and offski.*" He pointed Jake into the main shop and followed.

Where they stopped. And stared. Nothing had been locked away in the safe. Every display cabinet was full. And spotted a huge bunch of keys lying on the counter next to the till. Frowned a, *"what the fuck?"* at each other. Shook their heads and spread their hands in puzzlement. Jamesy went behind the counter to check the till. Stopped. *Psst!* Waved Jake over and pointed down.

At the body of what they assumed was the owner lying on the floor. No blood, no obvious injuries, no sign of violence at all. But no sign of breathing either. Jamesy checked for a pulse. Nothing. Jake raised his eyebrows in silent question.

"Dunno. Heart attack or stroke, looks like," Jamesy said as he started to pull off the old man's gloves. Ultra-thin, suede-type material.

"What're you *doing?*" Jake asked, thinking this's like taking the shoes off a dead man.

"Prints, my son. Keep your hands in your pockets, don't touch a thing. Must be some more somewhere."

He opened a couple of drawers behind the counter and came up with an identical pair that he handed to Jake.

"Right," he said. "Small stuff. Watches, rings, earrings, necklaces, that kinda thing. And leave the price tags on so we got an idea what to ask for them."

They took watches by the dozen. They'd heard of Rolex, Breitling and Omega but the rest were a mystery - what the hell was a Jaeger-LeCoultre when it was at home? But the price tags told them they were more than worth taking. They lifted every piece of diamond jewellery they could lay their hands on, as well as anything with rubies and emeralds. They put it all in a couple of leather bags they found in what looked to be the owner's small office.

122

They were about to leave when Jamesy noticed the safe. Well, door wasn't locked so maybe….. He turned the handle and door opened. Couldn't see any jewellery or watches, but there was cash. Four bundles of tenners and twenties that he quickly stuffed into the leather bags. Too stunned to comment, they slipped out the back, locked the door after them and strolled off to the underground.

* * * * *

And that one score set them up. When they got back to Jake's place, they counted the cash first. Which came to exactly six hundred and eighty quid's worth. Result! Jamesy exclaimed as he handed Jake his three hundred and forty.

When they then added up the tags, they found they had almost two hundred and fifty thousand pounds worth of gear. Shop value, of course. But still an undreamed-of fortune. They stared at each other, wide-eyed, once they'd finished adding it all up.

"But how the hell do we get rid of all this?" Jake asked.

"A good fence, of course," Jamesy replied. Thought for a moment or two. "But not old Clarkey on the estate, he's small-time *and* he can't keep his trap shut. Gotta be somebody." He paused. "Don't worry, my son, I'll find us a proper one."

And he did. Through a cousin who was a proper, hardened, grown-up villain. Even took the stuff to the fence himself.

"So your faces won't get known at your age." He explained to Jamesy. *"Because you can't trust them. Fences. They're part of our world, but not exactly in it, if you know what I mean. We need 'em, couldn't do without 'em, but they're not to be depended on, they ain't. Drop you right in it with Old Bill if it suited 'em. Which it does, more times than not."*

And he didn't want a percentage either.

"Not from family. Ain't done. Never live it down, I wouldn't."

What they got was five shillings in the pound. Not much on the face of it, but a net return of sixty-two grand was more than enough for two young guys who had previously been dealing in small hundreds. After all, that represented forty year's earnings for your ordinary punter. But for them? A nice little bankroll to kick-start their business for real.

It allowed them to get involved in proper skulduggery. Serious robbing and thieving - with violence, sure, but never murder. That was never their game. And so they prospered. Their roughest edges were smoothed away as they matured but they already had a reputation as men who were not to be messed with because of the retribution they dealt out. And once formed, a reputation sticks.

As a result, they were never challenged in a way that might have caused them any embarrassment or grief. And they gained another reputation: that of a tidy little firm that looked after its own business and caused no bother to the heavier firms.

The 'Mr Bigs', those men at the top of the London criminal hierarchy, knew about them of course, but left them alone. Jamesy and Jake knew their place in the grand scheme of things, and they were respected for it. Same went for the local Old Bill. A few favours in the right places, a little cash to Inspectors and Sergeants here and there and they were safe as houses. No word of them was ever passed along to Scotland Yard or the bigger thieves of the Flying Squad.

They didn't link up with any of the big firms either and made sure they were never seen as any danger to them. No toes were stepped on because they never worked in anybody else's manor. Instead, they went south in search of their illegal gains.

The coast, mainly. The 'quiet' little towns like Brighton, Bournemouth and even Southampton. Places where they weren't known. Working on information received. Or set up in little B&Bs until they'd sussed what was worth the effort. And always quick in and out so that none of the local firms – or coppers - could suss who was at it.

They knew Heathrow airport was out of bounds because the big firms had that sewn up. Not just the high value cargoes that came in but also the baggage handlers. Fortunes disappeared from cases and bags before the days of CCTV. There were simply too many rich, easy, pickings available to let the little guys in.

But not Gatwick. Small maybe in those days, but they quickly realised that it was both growing fast and was still wide open - a gift shop for any firm prepared to spread a few quid around for the right information. And so, working with a very few trusted mates, they prospered even more. And they would have continued in that vein, with a spell in prison a real possibility, if Jamesy hadn't proposed to his young lady. Jake soon followed suit with his.

And when the inevitable marriage came along - a joint wedding with most of South London's criminal names in attendance - they hit the jackpot for the second time. Jake said that his gran had always told him that it was better to be born lucky than anything else and reminded Jamesy that "*be lucky my son*", was a common saying.

Before the wedding, they were buying their houses. Cash. The Estate Agent, who turned out to be a very savvy gent indeed, looked at the houses they wanted, the money involved, and arranged a meet in a local pub. Once he'd bought the first round he got straight down to business.

"*Look, I don't know your business, chaps, and I don't think I want to, but if you have spare cash of this order, I'd advise you to invest in property as well as buying your own places. Seriously. London prices are going to go through the roof in the next few years and they won't ever come back down. You really can't go wrong. Trust me, it's guaranteed. I'll tell you the areas to buy in - Islington, Kennington and Clapham to start with. Rent them for a few years, then sell when the prices have tripled or better - then buy more and more. You'll make fortunes without having to work for it.*"

Renting? Jamesy had said. No thanks, nothing but hassle, innit?

The Agent didn't miss a beat. Not at all, he'd said, my brother's got a nice little property management company. You pay a monthly on each property and they take care of everything. And our cousin's a solicitor. Very flexible, he is. Take care of all the legals. No worries at all chaps. You'll be able to put your feet up and live well. And safely, he'd added, almost with a wink. Almost.

Jamesy thought he'd discovered a kindred spirit. But again, Jake wasn't so sure. Where's the fun in all that he'd asked. Jamesy explained it to him. Laid it out.

"Look, my son, we keep going the way we are, we're gonna make a mistake somewhere along the line. Upset some people. People we can't apologise to. Can't say sorry and just waltz off. No. Upset those guys enough and we're gonners. And there won't be no crem or graveyard either for the ladies to bring flowers to every year. We'd just be dumped at sea or under new bridge pilings and I dunno about you, but I really don't fancy that."

Jake wasn't having it. "But what do you care? You'll be dead. Somebody switches your lights out it just goes dark. Who cares what sort of dark it is?"

"Yeah, p'rhaps. But even if that doesn't happen, we've been lucky so far, but we're gonna get nicked and I don't fancy that either. Ain't doing bird for nobody."

Jake grudgingly acknowledged the sense of that, not fancying the thought of doing time either.

"Jake, my son. You done everything in life you want to?" Jamesy asked. "'Cos I ain't. Not by a long shot. We gotta change. Yeah, I like things the way they are but they ain't gonna stay that way. Everything changes. Life, people, situations. And if you ain't ahead of the game, this game we're in, wind up dead. Which is why we gotta get out. Look, that estate agent guy, Terry, what he said made perfect sense to me. What about you?"

Jake said that it did. Reluctant but accepting. "Only makes sense if he's on the level," he said. "He straight, you think?"

"Straight?" Jamesy said. "Why'd we need a bleedin' straight agent? Bent's what we need. So long as he does right by us – and he wouldn't dare do anything else – we want him as bent as."

As ever, Jake saw the sense of it and agreed.

"Then let's do it," Jamesy said. "We can still have some fun, guarantee you that, my son."

So they checked the guy out, discovered he was indeed bent, but sound, and they did as he suggested. Over the next forty years, they bought property after property, rented them out and then sold at increasing profits.

Which they used, in part, to buy greyhounds and racehorses. "*Well, gotta have a hobby or two,*" as Jamesy put it. And didn't have to get their hands dirty again. Oh, they invested in some naughty business, helped fund a few good scores, but that was it. Cash up front and a nice pay out after. And in those days, larger amounts of money paid into the right hands made sure Old Bill carried on ignoring them. Not protection as such, just studied ignorance of what was going on.

128

Which meant they were never in any real danger of being nicked again. They were happy, the wives were happy, and the kids were more than happy, becoming typical, over-indulged brats who had everything they ever wanted, but had no clue as to the value of money, and even less interest as to where it came from.

And this carried on until, in their early seventies and totally brassed off with their greedy, grasping, and ungrateful families, circumstances changed, causing the two old friends to seek a new life. A complete change from London, England, and all that they were surrounded by and immersed in.

Slowly drowning in, as Jamesy put it. Or suffocating to death. So, very quietly, they settled all their business, sold all their holdings, transferred their money to Spanish banks and bought an apartment in Barcelona.

"Not the bleedin' Costas, that's the first place they'll look for us," Jamesy had said.

They dug out their 'alternative' passports, bought new mobile 'phones and arranged to leave. Telling their wives they were off for the day to watch one of their horses at Sandown, *"Don't wait up, we'll be late back, 'specially if it wins."*

They met up in the VIP lounge in Heathrow and flew out to Spain. All they left behind were the family homes, cars and more than decent sums in the family accounts. They knew the wives and family wouldn't have the wit to track them down and when they realised they'd been left comfortable, they'd quickly forget them.

None of the criminals they knew and worked would be bothered either. They'd left no open business, no debts to be settled and that was all those guys cared about. Careful planning was everything. And they'd been careful. And they knew that once they acquired deep tans, grew beards, wore hats and sunglasses, even close family members wouldn't recognise them.

When they settled into their first-class seats, touched and raised Champagne glasses shortly after taking off, the smiles were broad and real and their contentment was deep.

Since they were both very smart guys, they quickly learned how to say all the simple Spanish salutations. Hola, cómo está? gracias, de nada and other small phrases became second nature to them. Before long, they sounded Spanish when they delivered them. And they quickly learned to read the Spanish menus in the non-touristy restaurants.

They used the same few bars, restaurants and beach bars and since they were polite and grateful to the all the bar and waiting staff - and tipped well - they quickly became liked and accepted. The fact that many of those staff assumed they were two elderly gay gentlemen caused them much amusement.

The day they realised it, they both burst out laughing.

"'Allo darlin'," Jamesy said, "gissa kiss, then."

"Sod off you," said Jake, and they both burst out laughing again.

The life suited them perfectly. Since they'd had all the excitement they'd wanted in their lives, this comfortable, quiet, slow-paced life was exactly what they needed. And the weather of course. That lovely sun. Even when it rained, it wasn't like London rain. Softer and warmer somehow. So even the rainy days didn't bother them.

* * * * *

Jamesy woke next morning, showered, shaved and did his few gentle stretching exercises. Then he dressed properly as he always did - no shorts and t-shirts for this man, despite the climate - and went through to the kitchen to make the coffee and dig out the pastries they always had for breakfast.

"Jake, coffee's up!" he called. But got no reply. He shouted again but still got no response.

Puzzled, he checked out Jake's room and saw that his bed hadn't been slept in. Fallen asleep, pissed, on the terrace again, he thought. Something Jake did at times. But not Jamesy. Old habits died hard. He liked his silk pyjamas, his bed and duvet too much - with the air conditioning cranked up.

He opened the sliding glass doors to the balcony and there was Jake, still lying in the recliner, the bottle of Brandy almost done. He reached over and shook his friend's shoulder.

"Wakey, wakey, Jake, my son. Sun's up and the coffee's brewed."

No response. He went to shake him again. Nothing. And then it suddenly hit him. Hit him very hard indeed. Ah Jesus, Jake, not like this.

Not now.

No, no, no.

Tears started rolling down his face with the realisation that the cancer had taken his friend months earlier than they'd been told it would.

I wasn't prepared for this, he thought, as he gently kissed the top of Jake's head and squeezed his hand. Acknowledging that almost seventy years of love and friendship had finally ended on this sun-filled balcony in Barcelona.

BLUES AROUND MIDNIGHT

The divorce had been easy. Easy in the process, I should say, not in the emotional sense. My ex-wife and I had handled it all like mature, sensible adults. There were no fundamental disagreements and no savage arguments which meant that solicitors were never involved. Between us, we put together an agreement on the division of assets and custody arrangements that was simply rubber-stamped by the Court.

Division of property was easy. I already owned the house when we got married and she didn't want half the value or anything like that. And wanted very little from the contents. The custody arrangements were equally easy to agree because she didn't want to take our daughter, Lizzie, with her.

Emotionally, well, that was a very different matter. Rejection is never easy, no matter how obvious it is that a relationship isn't working, and never will work, to the satisfaction of either party. And while it was obvious, it was equally difficult to accept. The heart is even less trustworthy than the brain in those situations.

Nevertheless, I had eventually reached a place that was at least manageable. In the simple processes of life, that is. But suddenly becoming the parent of a young daughter without an instruction manual was proving considerably more difficult. And that night was a perfect example.

I don't know how I heard her but as I lifted my head from the table, my daughter was standing there in her pyjamas. She looked at the crushed Guinness cans beside the remnants of a bottle of Jamesons and shook her head.

Because I did not handle the nights well. Work was a diversion, and the weekends and early evenings were full of Lizzie and our life together. But once she had gone to bed, the world seemed to close in around me in a way that was not comforting. Sometimes I thought, almost felt, I could hear a humming noise in the house, like a slow bass line resonating softly through an old Blues tune. I played a lot of Blues at night, Lightning Hopkins and Etta James in particular, because I found they were strangely therapeutic when I was feeling down.

But sometimes when I mixed the music with alcohol, it worked the other way and took me so far down I couldn't drag myself out of it and make it up to bed. Those were the nights I slept with my head on the kitchen table and woke with the imprint of the oak on my cheek. My *'wood face'*, Lizzie called it.

"Have I done something to make you sad, dad", she asked, that night, not moving any closer to me.

"What? No! Why do you ask? And what are you doing downstairs at two in the morning anyway? Why aren't you in bed asleep?"

"Because you told me last time when you got really drunk you only did it when you were sad and there's only me and you here so I thought I'd done something to make you sad and I woke up and went to get in your bed but I haven't wee'd my bed but you weren't there and when I heard you snoring I came down to see where you were."

I was always amazed that at eight, she could remember adults' ridiculous multiple questions. And answer them all, including the ones I hadn't directly asked. Even if she did often speak in those breathless, unpunctuated sentences that so many children use.

"Hey, no. You haven't done anything, Lizzie," I said. "You couldn't, sweetheart. Not to me. No. You're my number two, remember? My Two."

She had created this months ago. I was number one, because I was the grown up and she was the child and therefore number two. When I protested that she was *my* number one, she gave me a look I hadn't seen since my grandmother, and with unanswerable child's logic told me that we simply couldn't have two number ones and since I was already One, she was Two.

"No, I said, "I was tired after the park today, so I had a drink or two and the music just sent me off to sleep. That's all."

But she was aware beyond her years. She had seemed strangely grown up from the moment she started walking. There was none of the usual tottering around, bumping into things and falling over, just a determined little stride that took her exactly where she wanted to go.

135

I used to watch her with envy since I was, and still am, one of life's staggerers and weavers, constantly surprised that I've arrived anywhere without harming myself, or anyone else, along the way. And since her mother had left, she had become perfectly tuned to my moods and able to see through all my attempts at deception.

"Did mummy 'phone you again?" she asked, "because I heard the 'phone ring earlier."

I can never understand how children get through to the heart of it all more quickly and directly than any adult or therapist. But I'd learned very quickly that the truth was the best, and easiest way with Lizzie.

"Yes, she did."

"What did she want tonight?"

"She just wanted to know when would be a good time to come back and get the rest of the things she left behind. And to find out how you are, of course."

"So she knows when we won't be here," she said. A statement, not a question.

"She has to ask you, so she knows where to find the key."

I'd changed the locks a week after her mother had left, as soon as Lizzie told me *he'd* been in the house more than once when I was away on business. Though how Lizzie knew her mother no longer had a key I couldn't begin to understand.

"And I bet she didn't ask about me either. She doesn't care."

Another flat statement with no trace of emotion. Kids can be deadly.

"Of course she cares," I said, although I wasn't sure whether I believed that any more.

"You always say '*of course*' when you're fibbing, dad. And I know she doesn't care. She didn't want me, remember?"

"It wasn't that she didn't care about you, Lizzie, or that she didn't love you anymore. It was me she didn't like. Me she didn't want to be with. I told you at the time that me and your mum didn't love each other anymore, she loved somebody else, and so we'd decided it would be better if we lived in different houses."

She shook her head. "But she *didn't* want me, though," she said. "Didn't want to take me with her, did she?"

I started to speak but her look stopped me.

"Jess Moore's mum took Jess with her when she stopped liking her dad," she said. And David Walker's and Mollie's did. But they still see their dads at weekends, but mummy never sees me. *And* their mums are always going on about how bad their dads are but you never say anything nasty to me about mummy."

How could I explain to her that I couldn't say anything bad about her mum? That I was also responsible for what had happened? I was suddenly desperate for a cigarette and a large Jamesons. But I had a rule that I would never smoke or drink around her anymore and I wasn't about to break that now. No matter how badly I thought I needed it, I'd found that nothing was worth breaking promises or agreements with young children. And I always forgot how many children are in this same situation these days. And how much they all talked about it together.

"Hey Lizzie." I opened my arms to her but she didn't move. "Mum was just trying to be kind, you know. She thought I could take better care of you. And she knew you didn't like her new man, so she thought you would be happier here with me. That way you wouldn't have to leave all your friends, this house, your school, and you and me would have fun just like we always did."

Which was partly true. My wife had said those things to me and I knew she meant them. Because she'd never been very close to Lizzie. Didn't spend much time with her once she could be bottle fed and my lack of breasts weren't a hindrance. And never took her out, anywhere, just the two of them. She said more than once that she wished she had more maternal feelings, *"whatever they are"*.

We came home from the park one day when Lizzie was about five and she said:

"I see those other mothers with their children and I've realised there's something dislocated in me, or more likely something missing altogether. I just don't get it. The whole motherhood, child-fixated thing. I hate myself for it, and I've tried, believe me I've tried, but there's nothing I can do about it. I wish I could be more like you. Growing up with your two little sisters like you did, it just seems to come so easy to you.".

She was right, it did. And she said it with such regret and sadness in her voice, that I couldn't help but accept her inability to form any deeper relationship with Lizzie.

What we never discussed was the fact of how much that inability had an effect on our own relationship. She never raised it and I was never brave enough, or felt secure enough, to broach the subject with her.

But thanks to one of her friends who seemed to relish telling me, I also knew that her new man had said: '*No way. You have to choose between me and the brat*'.

And she chose him, of course, because it wasn't a difficult decision for her. Because it meant no more little   girl to prevent them taking off for a weekend when they wanted to. No more searching for 'child-friendly' holidays. No more PTA meetings to attend and educational development to worry about. No more sleepovers to organise. No more interrupted evenings, white wine going warm and sex going cold.

Lizzie waited until I brought myself back to the present. She smiled a sad, little smile. "It's okay, we'll be fine you know… *Woodface*."

And turned to go back to bed. I thought I couldn't possibly love her any more than I did at that moment.

I heard her shuffling back upstairs as I poured the last remnants of the Jamesons, lit a cigarette, put the headphones on again and let Etta James's '*Hush Hush*' smooth my brain back together.

THE LOVE ME SERIES

LOVE ME

The man and woman danced a slightly drunken, slow dance together. Close, but not too close. To any of the others who might have noticed, they just looked comfortable. Two old friends sharing a dance.

After a minute or two the woman moved her head a little closer.

"Do you love her?" she whispered.

There was a slight pause before he said, "Yes, I suppose I must. After all, I did marry her."

"Love her enough to keep you from leaving her then? To make you stay?"

He almost stumbled, the question was so unexpected. He looked down at her for the first time.

"Yes. I think I do," he said after yet another pause. They danced in silence for a while longer.

"So. Do *you* love *him?*" he asked. "Enough to keep *you* from leaving *him?*"

She laughed. And pulled him a little closer in.

"Most of the time, yes I do."

"And?"

"Yes," she said. "Enough to make me stay. *Most* of the time, anyway."

The music stopped and they parted, each going back to their own separate tables.

141

They never had another conversation quite like it. Never again referred to that night, that one dance. And despite everything, the man never left his wife until the day he died. But he often thought about what they'd said that night. And what had been left unsaid.

LOVE ME DO

The man and woman sat together in the basement bar of a pub in Soho. They were sitting side by side, but slightly apart. There was no touching, no hands on arms or knees together below the table but there was an air of closeness and warmth about them. Like new lovers after an unfamiliar act. They were both smoking.

"Is this all there is?" he said after a while.

"What?"

"This. Just meeting you for a drink each time we meet up in London?"

"Well, you could take me for a meal sometimes I suppose. A nice restaurant, just for a change. There are lots in London you know."

"No, not me," he said. "I don't do meals and restaurants much."

"You eat to live..."

"Rather than live to eat, yes, that's about it." He took a mouthful of his pint. "It could be more, though. If you really wanted. You only have to say the word."

"No, Michael," she said. "No, it couldn't. Because we're both married. Remember? And I'm not opening the cracks. You know they exist; I told you that a long time ago, when we first started seeing each other. But small cracks is all they are right now and that's how they're going to stay. And I offer no apologies for that."

He looked at her and grinned.

"Doesn't mean you couldn't come back to my hotel room, though," he said. "That would just be sex. Pleasure for pleasure's sake. You know. It wouldn't have to damage the rest of your comfortable bloody life, small cracks and everything."

"It just might, though," she said. "And I'm not sure I'm willing to take the risk. Not yet, anyway. And *just sex* you said?' Not much of a compliment that, is it? You might even call it an insult." She shook her head. "Just sex, indeed. Good lord."

"Okay," he said. "Well, if you ever do change your mind you will let me know... yes?"

"Of course I will."

The woman played with her vodka and tonic. She was small and dark but with surprisingly large breasts. She had met him straight from the conference and was dressed for business in a dark blue skirt and jacket and a cream shirt. The man wore a dark grey suit, collar and tie. Which was still fastened in place. The overall impression was executive, but his face and eyes suggested something quite different.

The woman tapped him on the arm and he turned to look at her.

"But, whatever, thank God for the affection," she said.

"What?"

"The affection. Between you and me. Between us. Don't you feel it?"

The man looked slightly puzzled, as if affection wasn't something that was familiar to him. An alien concept. Which, in fact, it was.

"Yeah, I suppose I must. I wouldn't keep meeting you otherwise. It's not a word that's usually in my vocabulary, though, affection," he said, repeating the word as if trying to familiarise himself with it. "Is it important?"

"Important? Oh my god, yes. Real affection is the heart of it all. The rest, including lust, which you know all about, is just padding."

"But there is no rest with us. I don't understand what you're trying to say."

"Don't worry about it. Even if there were more, it would just be padding, that's all."

The man looked at her. Thinking he would never understand women. Never had and never would.

"I'll take your word for it," he said.

"You'd better."

LOVE ME AGAIN

The man and woman lay in bed together in his hotel room in London. They had met up at five o'clock after the business meeting they'd both attended and had come straight to his room. They lay quietly after their second love-making session, her dark brown hair spread damp across the pillow.

"Are you thinking about it again," she asked, snuggling into him with her arm across his chest.

"That's all I can do… think about it. Especially after what we've just done. You and me together, permanently, I don't know, it just seems more real, after times like this."

"Unreal, you mean. Just you and me, great sex and the rest of the world locked outside the door. It's ideal, yes, but it's not real. Life just isn't like this, Michael. The reality would be you and me together dealing with everything that life could bring us."

"In between great sex, though," he said.

"That's if it stayed great through everything," she said. "And I can't be sure that it would."

"I know, I know," he said. "I get that, totally. The thought is so appealing though, you have to admit."

She snuggled into him and laid her arm across his chest, one finger absent-mindedly circling his nipple.

"Well… the only way anything more could happen is if you were to leave her. You know. And then I could leave James. If I left him now, I doubt he'd even notice. Pretty sure he wouldn't, to be honest. I don't even have to make excuses any more about being late back when you and I get these opportunities. Whatever the time I get in, he just accepts that when I'm back, I'm back."

Ha stared at her, eyebrows raised.

"He never asks you where you've been?"

"Never. Either he thinks I've been working late or been for a drink with people from work." She paused. "Or he doesn't ask in case he gets answers he doesn't want to hear. Either way, apart from the domestics, cooking, cleaning and shopping I mean, I'm pretty sure he wouldn't miss me if I did go."

"He hasn't got another woman, has he? Maybe that's why he doesn't seem to care."

She laughed out loud. "*James??* You serious? Because I can tell you, he hasn't. Would take way too much effort for him to take on another woman. He has no idea how to cope with me, never mind take on another one. No. No. No. He's faithful through lack of effort if not through lack of desire. That's the funniest thing you've ever said to me."

"You know I just couldn't do that," he said. "I wouldn't like to feel responsible for what she might do if I left her for good."

"You've said that to me before, but what could she do? Really. People divorce all the time. You'd go through the normal process, sort out the property, possessions, custody arrangements, the usual stuff, then it's over and you get on with your lives. And I've told you we wouldn't have to move in together, not at first."

"Yes, I know, but you don't understand. Nobody does. You've met her a couple of times, but you don't know her. Don't know what she's capable of."

"All I do know is that all the people I know, hardly any of them like her. Most of them can't stand her."

"I don't like her myself anymore," he said, "been a long time since I did. But she's my wife... and the mother of my kids. And that's what worries me."

"You hinted about this the last time," she said. "Tell me. Explain what you mean."

"Really?"

"Really. I want to know."

He eased himself away from her, sat up and put his arms around her shoulder. And lit them both cigarettes.

"Okay. Well, what it is, I'd be too frightened about what she'd do. She'd kill me for sure. And you. And she might just kill the kids and then herself. Just to keep things neat. Complete. Because her brain's so small she can't cope with disorder, chaos. If she isn't in control of something, *everything*, she doesn't know what to do. So she's more than capable of doing all that, doing away with all of us and think of it as just tidying up."

She propped herself up on one elbow and stroked his cheek. "My God, you're serious, aren't you?"

148

He nodded. "Deadly serious. If you'll pardon the pun."

"Yes, Michael, you've never been a man for overstatement or melodrama, have you. Certainly not at work. Or with me, come to that. But d'you honestly think she'd do all that? Really?"

He shrugged and stubbed his cigarette out.

"Well... maybe not all of it. Maybe not her and the boys. I don't know. She's certainly capable of it. But me? Oh, she'd kill me for sure. Absolutely. You as well, if she found out you were the other woman. And it wouldn't take her long to find that out."

"That frightens me," she said, "because you make it sound as if she's mad."

"Yes, I think she is. Completely deranged. Seriously, I do. The way she has to control everything. The house, the boys, and me... she thinks. Takes it down to the craziest levels. Drives me absolutely nuts."

"Really? Give me an example."

"Okay, how about this? Every time I go to watch United, she does me a bacon sandwich. Makes me sit at the dining table, won't let me have on my lap watching the TV football programme. Then, as I leave the house, she hands me a packet of wine gums *and* tells me not to eat them all in the car but to save some for half time. I'm so bloody sick of wine gums, I give them all to the young lad who sits in front of me. How about that?"

"Unbelievable. But she doesn't suspect anything? About us, I mean."

"Christ no. Not a chance. I'm one of the little bits of perfection living inside this idealised bubble she's created for herself. The only time she worries I'm slipping the leash is when I go drinking with my old mates. Always finds some stupid way of punishing me. But I don't do that much now, hardly see any of them anymore, she's made sure of that. No, she'd never imagine I'd ever have an affair. Couldn't allow herself to, really. Shatter the whole illusion she'd built up around being married to me."

"So *we're* okay then? We can still meet up when you come to London?"

"Oh yes, no worries about that. None at all. You're like a sanity drug for me, you are."

"Thank god for that. I can put up with him if I can still see you. Keep the lid on my own personal desperation."

They kissed and made love for a third time before she had to go.

LOVE WHISPERS

Two years later, the man and woman sat in a restaurant in Soho. They sat on their own at the table in the window. Separated from people at the other tables not just by physical distance, but also by an undefinable mood.

The man could, at times, be attentive and affectionate, loving even, but he was not a perceptive or observant man. Profoundly lacking any empathy, he simply didn't care enough about other people to be any of those things. It wasn't until he noticed the woman wasn't eating that he realised something might be wrong.

"You're not eating." He said, his own knife and fork poised in mid-air.

"I'm not hungry," she said. Not looking at him.

"Oh. It's just that we were in that meeting all afternoon and they gave us nothing but coffee. Thought you'd be starving."

And that was it for him. He carried on eating.

"Normally it would be," she said.

"*Normally*? So what's not normal?"

"The things that kill your appetite," she said. "No matter how hungry you are. Those things. They're what's not normal."

"And what would they be?" he asked between mouthfuls.

"Not a *they*, in this case, Michael" she said. "It's an *it*."

"Oh. And what is *it* then?"

"Us."

He finally stopped eating. Put his knife and fork down and stared at her.

"*Us?*" he said. Surprise in his voice. What d'you mean *us? I don't get it."*

"What other *us* is there, Michael? I mean us, as in you and me."

"Yes, okay. I get that. But what about us?" he asked. Still puzzled.

The wine waiter, who'd been hovering with a fresh bottle thought, '*She's dumping you, you silly arse and you don't get it . . . yet.*'

And no, not right now with the wine, he thought. He turned and raised his eyebrows to the two couples sitting at the nearest tables before walking away. Told the rest of the waiters to leave the couple in the window alone.

The other couples didn't turn their heads to look as they strained to hear the conversation next to them. In the way that people do when they have no conversation of their own. If they had looked, they would have seen the woman shaking her head.

"You keep saying *us,* Michael. But the simple fact is we're just not *us* anymore," she said. "We haven't been *us* for a long time now. Not in the real sense, I mean."

"*What?* I don't understand. I don't get you. What d'you mean, not *us* anymore? We're here, you and me, together again, aren't we? And we'll be going back to my hotel afterwards."

"Yes we would. And we would. Normally. And we'd have sex again instead of making love. Again. And again, and again. But what I'm trying to tell you, Michael, is that there won't be another *again*. Because no, I won't be going back to your hotel with you tonight. And we won't be having sex again. Because it's finished. It's over, Michael. I'm finished with the *us* we once were."

"Over? Finishing it? I don't understand what you're saying. Why? Don't you love me anymore? I thought you loved me."

"Love is a word we use in our own different ways. But yes, in the way you mean it, of course I still love you."

"Then why? If you still love me, why end it? He said, desperate now. "I *really* don't understand. Has your husband found out about us or something? Is that it?"

She shook her head in frustration yet again and took a long drink of wine while she gathered herself.

"Why must it always be for some external reason? Some other person... or *thing*? Why can't I make a decision myself? *For* myself. For no other reason than I've finally realised I need something different. It's what I want. What I *need*. What is so wrong with that?"

"I don't know how you could do this to me,' the man said. "Without any bloody warning either."

"Listen to me, Michael, please? Because I need you to understand. For once, this is not about you. I'm not doing it *to* you, *against* you, I'm doing it *for* me. There's a difference. All the difference in the world, actually. It's got nothing to do with you in that sense... you see, I'm leaving James as well."

153

"*What?* But I thought… Oh hang on, you've met another bloke, haven't you? Got something else going on, eh? Aah, yes, that's what this is all about, isn't it? Why can't you just come straight out and admit it instead of spouting all this personal growth stuff?"

She lowered her head until it was almost touching the table. Then straightened up and looked at him.

"Oh god. You're not listening to me. I suppose I could've made it easier for you, easier for you to understand, if I'd told you I *had* met another man. Maybe I should've done that, told you that's what it was and spared myself all this. But why should I? Because for once in my life it's about *me*. About what *I* want and need. And just as importantly, about what I *don't* want and don't need any more. Not about what other people want *from* me. And take from me. I've finally woken up, Michael."

But he wasn't listening. Or simply didn't understand what she was saying to him.

"Is the sex no good anymore, is that what you're saying? You don't enjoy it anymore?"

"Jesus *Michael!* Why does it always have to be about a man's erection and sexual performance? It's got nothing to do with the sex we have. Good as it's been, as it still is, it's just the icing on what is now a very over-baked cake. And anyway, half a dozen times a year? Be difficult to get bored with that, wouldn't you say?"

"But why leave him? He asked. " I thought you said he was perfect. Always passive and accepting. Never imagined you would ever have an affair so you could basically do whatever you liked. That's what you said."

"You're right. He was. Not a clue where you and I were concerned. I could come and go as I pleased. As I said, he didn't seem to notice."

"So why, then?"

"Because of my life, Michael. Or non-life I should say. I see you maybe those half a dozen times a year when you come to London and that's the only time I feel alive."

She paused and took a long drink of wine. What she desperately wanted was a cigarette, but it was years since that had been allowed in restaurants. And if she went outside to have one, she would lose the momentum.

"The thing is, Michael," she said, home is just a living death. Every day is the same emotionally. James does *nothing* for me anymore. There is nothing interesting, nothing amusing, nothing loving, nothing *different* about him anymore. He bores me. I've heard all his stories, all his life stories, and once you've heard every one of someone else's stories, what's left, really?

"I have to say that's a bit cynical," he said, shaking his head. "There's an awful lot more to relationships than that."

"Oh really? And what would you know about it? Be honest now. With me in one little box, to be opened when you want and your wife in another, managing the home and kids, you don't have to think about emotions, only processes."

"Processes? What are you on about?"

"The practical things in life, Michael. All you have to think about is, '*Where am I working next week? When do I see her? Where do we stay and for how long? Where should we go on holiday this year? When am I playing squash or football? When does the car need servicing?*' You know, that sort of thing. You never think about emotions or real care and affection."

He didn't respond. Couldn't. Just shrugged and stared over her shoulder into middle distance. She shook her head and took another drink of her wine. He just doesn't get it, she thought. Doesn't understand a word I'm saying.

"I honestly feel I'll die if I stay," she said eventually. "Die a long, lingering, suffocating death. And I'm only thirty-eight. I'm not ready to start walking down those stony steps to the grave. Seeing you these times has been enough 'til now. But it isn't any longer. The gaps are too great, my expectations are less each time and the excitement and pleasure have diminished bit by little bit."

"But that's not my fault, is it?" You're punishing me for something I haven't done," he said, whining like a wronged teenager. With a facial expression to match. She had a sudden urge to reach over and smack it. But composed herself instead.

"Think of it however you like, Michael," she said after a long pause. But I've come to realise that seeing you just doesn't compensate any more. After each meeting I used to just live for the next one. But I don't anymore. And you know what?" she said, pointing her knife at him. "The saddest thing is you're in danger of becoming nothing more than a *slightly* more interesting, *slightly* more exciting version of James and I really would hate for that to happen. That's why it's over Michael. Why it has to be for me at least."

156

"But we'll still see each other when I come to London. With work I mean. We can't avoid that. How will you cope?"

"I'll cope very well, thank you, since I'm leaving my job as well and won't see you at work ever again. As for you, I can't do anything about how *you* will cope. That's entirely up to you."

"Leaving?", he said, genuinely astonished. "To do what? How can you when you've never done anything else except work in the bank?"

"Well, thank you for that, Michael. I have a friend who is expanding her interior design business and she needs an office manager, a business manager, really, that she can trust. Someone who can effectively run the financial side leaving her free to do the artistic, the innovative side. What?" she said when she saw the look on his face. "Are you saying I don't have the skills for that?"

"No, no, of course you have. It's just that it's so different. It's not banking is it? And it won't be as secure, will it?"

"Secure," she said with a snort. "What you call security I call imprisonment, Michael. Boredom. Part of breaking away from you and James is getting rid of anything that *is* secure. Deathly secure. I want new. I want different. I no longer want the world of male bankers. And yes, you can take the rhyming slang as read. Don't you understand? I want interest. I want fun. I want *life!* If you can't see that, if you can't even imagine *yourself* breaking away, then I can't help you. Actually, I don't know that I *want* to help you."

157

Because you should have broken away years ago, she thought. Existing in that toxic marriage all these years has stripped away everything that was good about you. We never really had a chance once you decided to stay.

His response stunned her.

"I've never had you down as a feminist before," he said, raising his eyebrows and shaking his head.

"A *feminist?* Why do you men always need a label to help you understand things you haven't a clue about? There's no *'ism'* involved here, Michael. It's just me, a woman, deciding what is best for her. I want to create a life for myself which nourishes, develops and *frees* me. Why can't you accept that?"

There was a lengthy silence. She stared at him, trying to make eye contact but he just kept looking down at his plate. Eventually, he raised his head.

"You know I can't leave her."

She shook her head. Slowly. Wondering how you ever get a man to listen properly. To stop him making it all about *him*, every time.

"Yes, I know that, Michael. You told me that a long time ago. More than once, in fact. And I'm not asking you to leave her. I don't care if you do or not. No, *actually*, I don't want you to. I'm pretty sure I'd never be free of you if you weren't still locked in to all that."

"So, what will you do... apart from this new job that is?"

"I don't know, and that's what's so wonderful. Because I can do anything I want. There'll be nobody there to tell me what I can and can't do. Don't you see? For the first time in my whole bloody life, I'll be able to make decisions for myself. The big ones and the small ones. Change my lover. Change my job..."

"I don't ever remember you being that adventurous before."

"That's because I wasn't, Michael. You and James, between you, I began to feel suffocated, numbed almost. For years, I couldn't see past you and what was happening with the three of us. I was so busy concentrating on my job, my marriage and you, I couldn't see anything else. Couldn't see that I had options. *Or* that I could change things. *Me?* Making big decisions? Changing my world for *my* reasons? It just never occurred to me."

"It did though... eventually."

"Because I woke up... eventually," she said. And couldn't suppress a smile.

"And what caused that, your '*awakening*' I mean?" Returning her smile with a scowl.

"You did, actually. The way you talked about her, your wife, *and* the way you were with me outside of making love. Like I said, I could see you becoming just another version of James."

"So, any more big changes planned, are there?"

159

"Depends on how you define *'big'*. Because these might seem small to you, but they're big to me. Because, if I want to, I'll be able stay in bed all Sunday morning with my iPad, scouring Amazon and eBay, credit card in hand. While drinking coffee and eating chocolate biscuits. Without anybody nagging me about it all.

He went to speak but she stopped him with a raised hand.

"And no more feeling guilty because I'm not up at half nine, makeup done, hair perfect, in the kitchen, preparing Sunday dinner. Just think, I needn't eat another sodding Yorkshire pudding or roast potato ever again. If I want to slop about all day in my joggers, I can! And, almost best of all, I'll even be able to hold the TV remote and choose my own programmes! Can you imagine *that*? What absolute bliss."

It was as if she'd never spoken.

"I just never imagined it would ever end," he said.

She sighed. "Yes," she said, almost to herself, "James doesn't listen either."

"What?"

"Nothing. Never mind. What were you saying?"

"I said I never saw my life without you in it. You're important to me remember. You're my sanity, you are."

Me meeting your needs again, she thought. Supporting yet another entitled, ungrateful, unaware man who simply expects that sort of thing from a woman as his right. She smiled again.

"Yes, I remember you telling me that. But I need to retain *my* sanity. And I can't do that if I'm living the worst of both worlds. I refuse to go insane because of you two."

"But even if you leave James, you can still see me when I'm here, can't you?"

"Don't be an absolute idiot, Michael. I've told you why not as simply as I can and if you don't get it I simply can't be bothered to explain it all again."

"But what will *I* do now?"

Who bloody cares, she thought as she pointed her knife at him again.

"Not to be too blunt, Michael, but that's really not my problem, is it? I've got enough change in my own life to cope with, to enjoy, without wasting time on you and your problems. Imagined or otherwise. You'll have to work it out for yourself, as I'm sure you will, eventually."

"But I don't know what I'll do."

Who cares, she thought? Certainly not me. Not looking after this one's emotional needs ever again.

"Yes, you do," she said patiently – while screaming internally. "You'll just find someone else. Probably a younger version of me."

"I *will?*"

"Of course you will. It's what you do. Be plenty of younger women in the bank more than happy to hook up with you. Especially since you're even more senior. Don't tell me you don't check them out anymore. You always used to even when you were with me."

That stopped him for a moment. Then he nodded.

"Yes, I suppose I still do. Habit I guess. But it won't be you, though, will it?"

"So what? It will simply be another woman who's happy to give you what exactly *you* want. When you want it. The same way I always did. I wasn't the first, remember, and I won't be the last. As I just said, it's what you do."

"You sound bitter."

"Ah, Michael, don't try to turn it around. I won't have you putting it on me. And no, I'm not bitter..."

"You sound it," he said. "Don't know what I'm hearing if it's not bitterness."

"And I'm telling you it isn't. What it is, I'm just weary, that's all. Tired of you, tired of James. Tired of my job and the people I work with. Tired of the commuting, the routines, the wasted time. Tired of it all. And once that takes hold, there's no way you can shake it off. You either have to change it completely or end up going mad."

"But you said you still loved me. Earlier on, you said that."

"Love is a whisper, Michael. You have to be close to hear it. We're just not that close anymore."

He had absolutely no idea what to say to that.

LOVE WHIMPERS AND DIES

Three years later the man and woman met by chance on Regent Street in London. It was beyond awkward. There was no eye contact only lots of shuffling feet and odd, nodding heads. But confirming nothing. Or maybe everything. It was a meeting of bodies but not souls. Neither of them seemed to know what to say or do. But both of them wishing they were somewhere, anywhere, else. The woman finally spoke.

"Well hello, Michael. This *is* a surprise. Place the size of London and we somehow manage to bump into each other, eh? Weird or what."

"Yeah. Hi," he said, laptop bag over his shoulder, hands in pockets and head down looking at his shoes.

"How are you?" she said, trying to look him in the eye. But he just lifted his head and stared past her. "Are you still with the bank?"

"Yeah, of course. Who else would have me at my age? Too old to change careers now. But I've been promoted a couple of times so just waiting for the inevitable downsizing and picking up a nice severance package."

She shook her head. No change there then. Always the practical, always the *processes* of life. Thank god I cast him adrift when I did.

"But you're okay, Michael? Things going well apart from work?"

"Oh, you know," he said with a shrug. "Same old, same old. I wasn't like you. I never did enjoy change that I wasn't in control of. What about you?"

"Yes, thank you. I'm good. No, I'm *very* good actually."

"Oh. Still employed by that friend of yours then, are you? What was it, interior decorating or something?" Not keeping the sneer from his voice.

"Actually, I was never employed *by* her, thank you. We were business *partners* as well as friends. She wasn't my boss. And no, since you ask, after about six months we agreed it just wasn't really working out for either of us. I'm self-employed now, working as a business consultant. Mainly financial. I advise start-ups and young companies, helping them develop robust, flexible structures and sustainable business models."

She laughed. "God, would you listen to me? That sounded like a bloody sales pitch. Sorry. But yes, I've almost got more work than I can handle. And no advertising or marketing either. All by word of mouth. It's amazing what that brings in."

"You must be raking it in then," he said. Resentment in his voice this time.

"You could put it like that. But more like comfortable, I'd say. Because I'm earning four or five times what I did at the bank."

"*Comfortable?* More than that I'd say. You must be pulling down more than me even."

"Yes, imagine that," she said, daring a smile. "The little woman earning more than you, eh? Amazing really."

He ignored that.

"Suppose you've got a bloke to go with all that as well, have you?"

"Yes, I have, actually. Just over two years now. Although that's not all I have. He's not my whole life. We don't live together, I mean. I've been very careful not to fall into *that* trap again. Kept my own place, my own space, my own time and it works really well for me. And for him. He's remarkably adult for a man."

He ignored that little dart as well.

"Yeah, well... so... happy then, are you, having a man exactly where you want him?"

"That's not *exactly* how I would've described it, Michael, but yes, of course I am. Wouldn't still be with him if I wasn't happy."

"Right. So he likes you with all the extra weight, does he?" Looking her slowly up and down but lingering on her breasts.

"Ah no, be nice now, Michael. Be nice, eh? You used to be once." She sighed. "But yes, I suppose he must, since he still can't seem to keep his hands off me."

"I can understand that though because I think about you naked."

"Whaat?" She took a sudden step back.

"When I think about you," he said, "I think about you naked. Seeing you now, the extra weight you have, I'll have to revise my mental image though."

Shocked, she took another step back and raised her left hand as if in self-defence.

"Do you have *any* idea how weird, how *creepy*, that sounds, Michael? And how typically bloody *male* it is. Your only memory of me is my naked flesh? *Jesus!*"

"So how do you think of me then?"

165

"I hate to disillusion you, Michael, but I don't think of you at all anymore. And if I ever did, I very much doubt your naked body would be the first thing that came to mind. Or the second."

"So you're saying it was all totally irrelevant then, all that, you and me?"

She studied his face. Was there some softening in him? Could that be self-pity in his voice, or resentment? Regrets perhaps? It's all of that she thought. But didn't say it. She stared past him as she answered.

"Not irrelevant, no, of course not. How could it be? But it's part of my past. Part of who I used to be. A part that helped to bring me to where I am. But it's not relevant now, because I am not that person anymore. I have a new life, Michael. *My* life. One I've made for myself, for me."

"You make it all sound so easy," he said.

"If you think it was easy, then you've less of an idea about life than I ever thought."

He didn't respond to that, and another silence grew. Neither of them looked at each other. But after a while, rather than simply turn and walk away, she spoke.

"So. How about you? Things any better at home?"

"No, they're not. Worse than ever to be honest. *She's* worse than ever. I'm thinking of having her sectioned."

"*What?*"

"Yeah, it'll be easier – and safer - than killing her. Fucking mental bitch."

"*Oh god!*" Her hand flew up to her mouth. "Well, I… I don't know… okay… well… bye then, Michael."

"Yeah. Bye."

Neither of them hesitated or looked back as they walked away.

LOVE NEVER AFTER

Another two years passed without the woman once thinking about him. Then, one evening, as she sat quietly surfing the news channels, a name caught her eye. The name of the bank where she had previously worked.

She scrolled quickly back and read the piece. And came across the name of the man who was the subject of the article. Michael O'Neill. Her Michael, as was. His name given in connection with complaints of sexual harassment in the workplace. Two of them involving inappropriate touching and groping, and one of attempted rape at an office Christmas party.

She noticed that all the alleged offences took place after her relationship with Michael had ended. Curious she thought. Never imagined he would become so desperate.

Once the accusations became known within the bank, three more women came forward with further complaints of inappropriate touching and physical harassment that stopped short of attempted rape.

Following an HR investigation, he was found guilty of gross misconduct, sacked, and denied his pension. Which his employers considered to be sufficient punishment.

But the women weren't satisfied with that. They found specialist lawyers who presented their case to the police and a further investigation took place. He was arrested, tried, found guilty and sentenced to eight years in prison.

For some reason she couldn't at first explain, she found she wasn't surprised. But then she thought back to the start of their relationship. And remembered that he had touched and kissed her – again at office party – without her invitation or consent.

But she hadn't objected or made a formal complaint. Because she was attracted to him. Fancied him something rotten in fact. Even if she hadn't, and had made a formal complaint, nothing would have been done. Didn't happen. Not back in those long-ago days.

Her only reaction was "well done those women".

And she wondered how she could ever have loved him. But stopped herself because she'd been a completely different person and the one she was today would never have accepted it.

Satisfied, she carried on surfing the news sites. And never thought of him again.

Originally from Newcastle, Ian is now happily retired and living in Bristol. He has 'scribbled' all his life, mainly for the pleasure of friends and family, but has only recently begun writing full-time. His personal motto is: *"You're never too old and it's never too late."*

Drawn from his broad experience of life, the stories in this volume explore many of the effects of human love. That "many splendored thing" that we all know but find it almost impossible to define. They examine the impact of finding love, keeping it and losing it, and the joy, pain, loss, anger and sadness that comes with it. They are a collective attempt to describe an integral and essential part of the human condition.

This is the second book in the trilogy - "It's The Human Condition".

Front cover image by Sandra Hutchinson Photography

Rear cover photograph by Susan Jean Photography

Printed in Great Britain
by Amazon